FROM THE FILES OF THE

OTHERWORLDER ENFORCEMENT AGENCY

VAMPIRE GAMES

TIFFANY ALLEE

Previously released on Entangled's Ever After imprint – October 2013

Entangled Publishing, LLC
2614 South Timberline Road
Suite 109
Fort Collins, CO 80525
Visit our website at www.entangledpublishing.com.

Covet is an imprint of Entangled Publishing, LLC.

Edited by Erin Molta and Robin Haseltine
Cover design by Curtis Svehlak
Cover art by DepositPhotos

Manufactured in the United States of America

First Edition October 2013

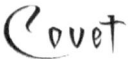

To Hillary. For all the things.

Chapter One

For once, it wasn't a nightmare that woke me. The booming knock at my door sounded again and I dragged myself out of bed. I held my gun at my side, out of view, and opened the door a few inches. "Yes?"

The man didn't appear to be armed, I'd give him that. But I was, even if it was my personal sidearm, and knocking so loudly before my alarm went off was almost enough to make me shoot him. But I was a professional. An agent with the Otherworlder Enforcement Agency. And shooting a man for waking me up before dawn would result in a heck of a lot of paperwork.

I hated paperwork.

By the looks of his expensive suit, obviously tailored to his lean frame, he wasn't delivering a package. But he had the slightly pale pallor of a vampire, which meant a standard-issue bullet would probably just piss him off unless I got in a really lucky shot.

My bleary gaze sharpened. Shock hit me as I studied the line of his jaw, and the paleness of his blue eyes. What the hell was *he* doing here?

"Beatrice?" His gaze slid down my oversized flannel pajamas as if my outfit wasn't quite what he was expecting. "Long time."

"Yeah." I fought the heat flushing my face but lost. What did I care what the bloodsucker thought of my pj's? It was five o'clock in the damn morning. What was I supposed to be wearing? Even agents got cold in St. Louis in March. "Why are you here, Claude?"

The Chicago detective ran a hand through his hair, and for a split second I could feel its softness sliding between my fingers.

"I need your services." He flashed me a grin, and I frowned at his flirting tone. Once upon a time I might have flirted back—okay, I definitely would have flirted back. But it had been a rough couple of weeks. A rough year. Ever since my former partner and I had worked a big case involving succubi being kidnapped and sold to the highest bidder, I'd struggled against dark emotions. I had seen too many horrible experiences, and I hadn't been able to let up or take a break from work for far too long. Lives had been on the line, succubi kidnapped and murdered.

It wasn't unusual for us to go through this kind of thing, hit a breaking point and need to slow down and take some time away. But I didn't like it. I was at my best when I was working, and there was always another criminal to take down.

"What kind of services?"

"Your services as a psychometrist, of course. I have

an object that I believe may carry a psychic imprint," he clarified, but his flirtatious grin didn't falter.

"No shit. Here I was figuring you'd stopped by to chat."

"Well, aren't you charming before your first cup of coffee?"

I didn't grin at his joke, but it was a near thing. Of course he was looking for my services as a psychometrist. Investigators didn't show up at my door at this time of night looking to chat. My ability to read the psychic imprints left on objects was at a premium these days. Not that my interpretations could clinch a case. Fact was, half the time my powers didn't work. True emotional trauma had to have occurred near the object for a psychic imprint—unless I was able to read something physically connected to a person, like their hair.

"You're a long way from Chicago."

The vampire was something of a legend among cops. As a member of the Chicago Paranormal Unit, he'd solved several high-profile crimes that had made the national news. And more than that, he was rumored to be high up in whatever private echelon vampires used out of the public eye.

"You're worth the trip," he said. Then, at my glare, he quickly added, "You're the best psychometrist in the Midwest."

"That's bull."

He blinked. "Excuse me?"

"I'm the best in the country." I gave him a lazy smile. Okay, maybe I was up to flirting a bit, even if seeing him still stung. Claude had shown his true colors long ago. "But that doesn't explain why you're here."

Especially considering that I wasn't, strictly speaking, on

duty for the next two weeks—if psych even approved me to come back then.

My gut twisted at the thought, but Claude laughed, and some of my tension released. The man was too damn pretty and, laughing, he was something else. Light brown hair topped his head, cut in a longish way that I suspected was designed to appear messy.

Of course, I knew the muscles that were only hinted at under that jacket were stronger than those of any human. I knew how they flexed and moved in the light. I knew how they felt under my fingertips.

"You are the best in the country. Glad to see you realize it." He stepped forward and leaned on the doorframe, slightly in my personal space, as if casually asking for a date. But I wasn't fooled, and I didn't back up. I could see the wariness in his eyes and the tension in his body. As if he was ready to be attacked at any moment. The Claude I knew was cool and collected—whatever he was here for, it was putting him on edge. This couldn't be good.

"I need a favor. I have some evidence that needs your special touch."

I glared at him. "You ever hear of something called a formal request? Or the fucking phone? Or, I don't know, waiting for daylight?"

"That all sounds terribly time-consuming."

"Well, that's the thing about doing shit the right way—"

"Please. It'll take five minutes. The official paperwork will get to you eventually—you know how long that can take."

I suppressed a sigh. Five minutes? More like two hours of paperwork once the official request caught up to me. But the man had come all the way from Chicago. And it was pretty damned unlikely he'd done that on a whim.

But I was over what had happened between us—not that there had been anything to really get over. And no matter that I jerked his chain now, I was always willing to help out another investigator. Besides, I was stir-crazy. I'd been away from work for two weeks already, and it was likely to be another two before I'd be back on duty—minimum. Annoyance rushed through me at the thought, but I pushed it down.

"Fine. But not here. There's a diner down the road." I gave him quick directions to the twenty-four-hour place. It would be almost empty this time of morning.

He grimaced. "This is kind of private—evidence and all."

"We'll be discreet. Or, we can go to my office. I don't bring my work into my home." Not purposefully anyway. It was my sanctuary. The one place I didn't have to think about death. Didn't have to see it, experience it. Not that my visions didn't follow me here—didn't follow me everywhere. But that didn't mean I had to invite them inside.

He shrugged. "As you wish. The diner sounds good. I'm a tad peckish." He flashed his teeth and headed down the sidewalk.

I glared after him, annoyed at the thrill that ran through me at seeing him. And worse, at the flash of his fang.

The last bit of winter clung to the St. Louis streets, seeping into my bones the second I stepped out of my house. The drive to the diner took less than five minutes—not long enough for the heater in my car to kick from cold to hot.

The diner door *dinged* as I opened it, then smacked the doorframe when I let it slam behind me. A man dressed in jeans and a heavy flannel shirt occupied one corner booth, nursing coffee. The large semi-truck taking up one side of the small parking lot no doubt belonged to him. I guessed the diner staff must not care about parking this early.

Claude had taken a booth on the opposite side of the diner from the trucker, hidden from view from the front door and off to one side of the counter where the waitress refilled the coffeemaker.

I sat across from Claude, noting he'd made sure to keep his back away from the front door. I was not so lucky. Then again, I wasn't paranoid enough to think someone was going to sneak up on me at this time of the morning. But I hadn't been alive long enough to gather the enemy list Claude probably had. Of course, he knew what I was like in the morning, pre-coffee. He might be right to be nervous.

"What can I get for ya?" The waitress looked like every man's grandma. Glasses perched on the end of her nose, and tightly curled gray hair touched her ears.

"Coffee, please." Claude gave the waitress a world-class smile, and she smiled back at him patronizingly, unimpressed with his good looks.

"Decaf for me," I said. The smell of bacon and eggs filled the air enticingly, but I refused to eat breakfast. That would be as much as admitting that I was up, and I was going back to bed the second I returned home. To sleep.

Hopefully, a dreamless sleep.

The waitress nodded and left, then returned with our coffee and a bowl of various flavors of creamers. I grabbed a couple of hazelnut packets and poured them into my cup.

"Thanks again for your help," Claude said. "How have you been, *mon chou*?"

"Dump the small talk, Claude." I resisted the urge to tug on my hair. How, after all this time, could the man make me immediately angry? The term of endearment pushed my buttons. It made me wonder what would have happened if things had ended differently. But it was an old wound I wasn't keen to reopen with what-ifs.

He reached for the creamer, his hand brushing mine slightly as I went for the sugar packs. A bolt ran through me, recognition and need merging with regret to form a ball in the pit of my stomach. I stilled, and slowly he pulled away.

"I'm not trying to anger you," he murmured.

"Then dispense with the pretty endearments."

He raised his eyebrows but didn't argue. From the seat next to him, he grabbed a rolled-up paper bag and slid it across the table to me.

"Not so fast. Give me some background info," I said. He frowned, so I added, "It'll help put the images I see into something that might actually make sense." And it would. But mostly, I didn't like to touch shit without knowing what I might be in for. Even for Claude Desmarais.

My resistance seemed to surprise him, but that made sense. Six years ago I'd been a bright-eyed, positive girl without a real clue about the world, and willing to go the extra mile for a smile of approval from a star among cops. And I'd had a hell of a crush. A crush he'd been more than willing to explore after just a bit of convincing on my part.

He was still a legend, and just as striking and ageless.

But I wasn't that girl anymore.

Claude paused for a moment, then nodded—more to himself than to me. "All right. There have been a series of murders back in Chicago. We think it's a serial killer."

"No OWEA involvement yet?" The Otherworlder Enforcement Agency was similar to the FBI in that we mostly waited until locals called us in.

"Not until you."

I grunted, keeping my opinion on the matter to myself. The Chicago Paranormal Unit—or PNU—was a good unit, but the OWEA had more resources.

"People have been disappearing. We've found several bodies thus far that seem related to the same guy."

"How many still out there that might be related?"

"No way of really knowing." He took a sip of the coffee and grimaced.

I sipped my coffee, relishing the hazelnut flavoring while I considered what he had said. "How do you know the deaths are related?"

"They were all branded using an honest-to-God branding iron."

I choked on my coffee. Claude handed me a napkin and I nodded for him to continue.

"The brand is in the bag—that's the evidence I need you to touch."

"Wait a sec." I took a deep breath and coughed again to clear my throat. "You managed to get the brand? How the fuck did you do that?"

The trucker passed our table, heading toward the men's room. He nodded in greeting, and I nodded in return.

Claude shrugged and lowered his voice. "Got lucky. The end must have broken off in the fire. We found it settled in some old ash."

I frowned. Something didn't jive with his story. Brands didn't just break off. Not that luck didn't help solve the occasional investigation—hell, routine traffic stops caught a shitload of criminals who'd done far worse. Of course, the vampire wasn't giving anything away. I was willing to bet the man had been able to lie easily since before I'd been born.

Not that he looked it. I was twenty-eight, but looked like I was in my early twenties—despite the stress inherent in my job. Claude looked a few years older than I did. But he had the poise of a much older person. And while I couldn't feel much of the signature vampire fear aura radiating from him, that didn't mean much. The intimidating aura that exuded from vampires seemed to have little to do with their power or age.

"Tell me the rest."

"I'm kind of on a timetable here. Tell you what, read the brand for me and I'll send you the file."

I let out a breath in a big whoosh of air. Truth was, I didn't want to handle the icky brand that had probably been used in some sort of sick, ritualistic murders. I didn't want to watch people die in my head. And I most definitely didn't want to carry that memory with me until the day I died.

But that was the job.

Granted, not a job I was supposed to be doing without authorization, but my skills were far too useful to the OWEA for them to fire me for skirting the line.

I nodded and he slid over the bag. I unrolled the heavy bag. It was a normal evidence bag, but it didn't have the normal tags. No case number. Nothing. That bothered me, so I made a mental note to check up on it later.

Air whooshed in and out of my lungs as I purposefully hyperventilated. I had passed out twice from lack of oxygen during a vision before I realized that such a simple thing could help.

I stuck my hand in the bag and gripped the branding iron.

A loud rush of sound filled my ears, as if I'd just plunged my head into a bucket of water. Inky darkness overtook my vision for half a second, and I fought sudden claustrophobia.

Every time, I experienced the same overwhelming feeling of being trapped in a dark, airless, white-noise-filled room. And I always tried to move—even knowing that movement was impossible.

Then the fear and sensory deprivation was gone. And what replaced it was worse—always worse.

Glowing with orange fire, what could only be the brand filled my vision. The symbol was unfamiliar. Five lines converged into a triangle, with a swirl cutting across the lines. Smaller symbols that looked like eyes peeked out from the spaces in between the lines.

A man's face replaced the brand. He frowned at me, and I had a difficult time focusing on him. My vision blurred. He was saying something, but I couldn't hear him. His frown deepened and he turned away, still talking. He wasn't talking to me. The realization seemed unimportant. Foreign emotions ran through me, too fast to identify them. But fear soaked it all. Fear and almost debilitating panic.

The metal edges of the diner table came into focus first, and I sucked in a breath of air. Then Claude asked if I was all right. I waved him off, trying to get my bearings.

"I'm fine," I managed. I wasn't really. I never was after a particularly violent vision. Not right after. Not even a week after. It took time for them to fade.

Luckily, this vision hadn't been terrible—of course, the initial one usually wasn't. Sometimes I witnessed the torture, the death. But something about this vision felt off. The man's face had almost seemed…familiar. And a sickness filled my stomach, as if the coffee disagreed with me.

I shook my head. Maybe the OWEA shrinks were right. Maybe these visions were getting to me.

I raked my eyes over the room, over the painfully handsome vampire sitting across from me in the booth, over the old and worn decor of the diner around us, over his tailored suit. I barely allowed myself to blink. It took my body a few minutes to stop shaking, and just as long for the sight of the solid room around me to convince my brain that I was no longer trapped in that cold place with the flaming brand.

Claude waited silently. Too silently. His eyes were on me, and his body betrayed no movement. Vampires did that sometimes. Creepy.

I broke the silence the way I always did, with my first impressions. "I saw the brand, then it went away and a man replaced it—a vampire. He said something—was talking. But not to me—the vic, I mean."

"What did he say?"

I raised my eyebrows at his question, but before I could come up with an appropriately smart-ass reply, he answered his own question.

"Of course. Psychometrist visions are sight-only. No auditory or olfactory." He leaned forward and a bit of his hair fell onto his forehead. "Anything else?"

Just sight-only impressions? If only. Not that *watching* murders happen from the point of view of the victim or murderer wasn't bad in its own right, but the emotions are what stuck with me.

What would I tell Claude? The victim was afraid as he was being branded? That the victim was beyond thinking, because he'd been tortured so long his pain became psychically linked to the brand used in his torture?

"Did you see anything interesting in the background?" Claude pressed.

"No. I rarely get anything from the background with a first pass. And sometimes the images just flash—a floating face, an object set against a black background. Some emotions." I shrugged and, finding my muscles tense, I rolled my shoulders. "It takes time and repeated sessions for me to get more of the picture."

He frowned at that. "Okay. Can you describe the man in the vision to me?"

I closed my eyes and recalled him as well as I could. "I can do you one better." Again my stomach turned when I brought the man's face to mind.

I pulled my sketchpad out of my oversized purse and drew the face I'd seen. A few quick swipes and I had a basic drawing done. I added some key features, lines around his eyes, and the way his hair swept across his forehead. The slight hint of fang amidst his perfect set of teeth. Then I stopped to look at it. My hand shook. I shoved my pencil back into my bag to cover my shaking fingers, then turned the picture to Claude. Closing my eyes, I took a deep breath. Something about the picture bothered me—probably just seeing the face in a vision that had turned so horrible, so fast.

A crunching noise made my eyes flutter open.

"You're sure?" Claude said, and I couldn't look away

from his expression. By all accounts, Claude was an old vampire. And old vampires were masters of controlling their emotions, of keeping their thoughts off their faces. But the wide eyes and tense set of the vampire's jaw was hardly controlled. Something about the picture surprised him. Something he didn't like.

I scanned the area for the source of the odd crunching noise. Had Claude heard it, too? "Yes. I'm sure. But if you let me keep the brand for a week or so, I can probably get you more."

"That won't be necessary." The vampire stood and gave me a short bow. "Thank you for your help. It was nice to see you again." He turned to go, then halted next to me. His hand closed around my shoulder and squeezed, and I couldn't help the small shiver that ran through me. "Really. I appreciate this, *mon chou*. And I am…happy to see that you are well. I wish—" He shook his head. "Thank you, again." Then, without another word or a backward glance, he was gone, with the bagged brand slipped under his jacket.

What the hell? I reached for my coffee and something on Claude's side of the table caught my eye. I slid out of the booth and walked to his side to get a better look.

My breath caught. Two palm-length imprints were etched into the smooth table. I took a long drink and then leaned down to look under the table. Sure enough, it looked like fingers had been dug into the particleboard underneath.

Claude had gripped the table hard enough to leave dents. That was the crunching sound I'd heard while showing him the man—the vampire—I'd seen in the vision. There was only one explanation that I could come up with.

Claude knew him.

Chapter Two

Squealing tires cut through the early morning stillness. Someone cried out, and a car door slammed.

I tried to see through the darkness, but I could only hear the laughter. I could only see the face, grim and sinister.

And then he was gone.

Bright light pierced my curtains when I awoke for the second time that day. My breath came fast, and I struggled with confusion.

I hadn't had this nightmare in years. Hadn't experienced the horrible dream that had plagued me as a child. But it was back. He was back.

And he wore the face I'd seen when I touched the brand.

Less than twelve hours later, I stepped into the elevator of Claude's opulent condo building, after the suspicious-yet-polite doorman received permission from Claude to let me up. The vampire might not live traditionally, but he did live in style. The building was set on Chicago's Gold Coast, the nickname locals gave the area of the city adjacent to Lake Michigan. The views were certainly worth the title, but the prices clinched it. A person practically needed a pile of gold to buy one.

The elevator ticked up the floors, and my temper ticked up with it. I half wished I'd brought my personal sidearm with me, but I wasn't too keen on explaining away why I'd brought a gun with me when I wasn't on a case. Or even on the job. Damn the vampire anyway. I wasn't supposed to be in Chicago. And I wasn't supposed to be running down a case that didn't even exist.

Anger was good. It grounded me when everything else felt surreal. But I tugged on my hair and tried to calm down. Fiery redhead was just too cliché. Had to keep a lid on the rage, although anger was far preferable to longing for something I couldn't have. After all, it was obvious that Claude struggled with no such emotion.

In my hand, I clutched the folded paper. The portrait of a psychotic killer. But I didn't need it.

I saw him every time I closed my eyes.

It was a face I'd seen for the first time as a ten-year-old girl in visions that had become nightmares. Ones just like the nightmare that had propelled me out of bed in the late morning straight onto a flight bound for Chicago.

A *ping* sounded as the elevator doors announced that I'd reached the penthouse. A short hallway revealed only a single door. How much had the vampire had to pay to avoid neighbors? Whatever. If I'd had centuries to accumulate wealth, I could live in a high-rise, too.

I'd not allow myself to be intimidated by a shiny apartment.

Dressed far less impressively than he had been earlier in the day, Claude answered the door. He was wearing an AC/DC T-shirt and jeans so worn they looked older than me. But this time, his expression wasn't open or friendly. Anger twisted his mouth, and his eyes looked weary. He gestured for me to enter, but I paused in his doorway, unsure for a moment what bothered me about him. I'd expected the anger. But I hadn't expected him to look so drained.

Vampires, as a general rule, just didn't look tired.

"You called the station to check up on me," he said. It wasn't a question.

"Of course I did. You showed up with an unmarked evidence bag and no paperwork, and you expected me not to check? What kind of an investigator do you take me for?" I ached to mention the man from the vision—the vampire. Claude knew who he was, that much was obvious. But there was direct, and then there was rude. And rude wouldn't get me the answers I so desperately needed.

And I wasn't so sure I should show my hand just yet.

Some of the anger drained from his expression, but the weariness remained. "You're right. I should have expected that." A hint of a smile touched his mouth. "Guess I'm a little off my game. Are you thirsty?"

I followed him to the living room and then sat on a plush leather couch while he went to get me a soda. Decorated in an understated style, the condo was lovely, if a bit plain. A few antique furnishings and paintings that offered to sweep me away to another place brightened the room and made up for the lack of other personalized touches.

And any plainness was made up for by the view. The lake stretched so far that a person might mistake it for an ocean. Dark blue and calming.

Claude swept back in, and I snagged a coaster from a small stack on one of the end tables to set under my glass. The coffee table wood was old and pitted, but in a purposeful style.

"So are you going to tell me what this is about?"

He raised an eyebrow at that, and the grin on his face never faltered. "What? No accusations of misconduct? No suggestions that I'm taking money on the side to investigate cases? What kind of interrogation is this?"

I shrugged. "You're a good cop, by all accounts. And I don't see you taking money on the side. Look at this place. Hell, you probably forget to cash your paychecks."

He laughed at that, and my mouth went dry. The man was more than attractive, with his intense eyes that belied his casual look. But laughing…damn.

So not fair to the women of the world.

The amusement drained from his expression when I only offered a small grin in return. At least, I hoped it looked like a grin and not a grimace. The man's laugh was infectious, but not infectious enough to overcome the tight chest and headache I'd been overrun with since waking up from that nightmare.

"And I feel like I know you, a little bit. I mean, we have worked together in the past," I added. I opened my mouth to tell him that he'd made an impression on me, and that I still thought of our time together, now and then. But I couldn't say that. It would betray too much, and make me sound like the naive girl I once was.

"But that doesn't mean I'm not going to ask you for an explanation," I said, instead.

"You need to leave this alone."

I shook my head. "Not going to happen." For more reasons than he realized.

Our eyes met and all the air left the room for a moment. Just being here, around him, felt unreal. My fingers itched to reach out and touch his skin, to confirm that he was really there, sitting so close to me, after all these years. Seconds ticked by, marked by a grandfather clock that stood in one corner of the room.

My throat tightened. I knew more about him from his reputation than I did from the time we'd spent together alone. Watching Claude now, his expression enigmatic and his motivations hidden behind his amused expression, it hit me that I'd never really known him at all.

"You need to let this go. It's a personal investigation, and it's unnecessary for the OWEA to be involved."

"You're the one who dragged me into this. Look…" How much to confide? I opened my hand, where I still clutched the picture I'd drawn. Carefully, I unfolded it. The face appeared, marred now by the folds and smudged because I'd drawn it up in pencil.

But my body's reaction was immediate and fierce. My vision closed up, and all I could see was that face. Snarling, fangs flashing. Dark eyes narrowing. I didn't realize how hard I was clutching the paper with the tips of my fingers until Claude tugged it from my grasp.

He didn't look at the picture. I guessed he didn't have to. Instead, he sat next to me, close enough that I could feel the slight coolness of his body. Vampires weren't as cool as salamanders, but they ran a couple of degrees colder than humans.

His closeness was somehow comforting, which was silly; I barely knew the man, no matter what I liked to think in the dead of night when I was alone. But my body disagreed, and I fought the urge to lean against him and, just for a moment, take comfort. Breathe in his scent. Feel his hands on my skin, while his body moved against mine. Let the real world slip away.

Like I had once before.

"Tell me," he murmured.

The full truth almost fell from my dry mouth before I could stop it. But I caught myself. "I'd like to help you, for old time's sake."

If it was possible, he grew even more still. "You can trust me, Beatrice." His voice was low, caressing, and far too close to my ear. Trusting him when he still hadn't confided anything in me — had in fact just lied to my face only hours before — would be stupid. No matter how much I wanted to.

It had been so long since I'd been able to trust someone like that.

I pushed up from the couch, unsettled. "I don't think so. I've already shown trust by not reporting your little side case. I'm offering you my skills as an investigator and a psychometrist — temporarily anyway. Don't look a gift horse in the mouth."

He considered me for a moment, expression sharp and thoughtful. "You're right. I guess if you can have that much faith in me…" He got up from the couch and paced back and forth across the room. "I'm after a killer, a man who has done horrible things. But he hides in the shadows. Using his name and connections and money to cover his trail."

"And you're not running this through your department because. . . ?"

"Just over a month ago, my partner was involved in a case with an OWEA agent while I was out of town on vampire business. The case involved a vamp homicide. Vic was killed on Luc Chevalier's — the Magister's — casino ship."

I'd heard about the case — a murder so closely connected to a Magister that it had made the national news. The details had been dramatic, with a lycan OWEA agent injured, and two of Chicago's finest losing their lives. Another Chicago detective had been at the heart of the case, too. A young woman whose face had made headlines alongside the agent for cracking the case.

"Holmes," I muttered.

"Yes. Astrid Holmes. My partner." Affection was obvious in his tone. He resumed pacing. "The case was all but tied to the Magister's son, Nicolas. But, once again, he wriggled free. All witnesses dead, and we were left with only circumstantial evidence to connect him. And that was flimsy."

Officially, vampires were guided by Magisters, who coordinated leadership and law enforcement with the official lawmakers. Unofficially, the vampires were rumored to have a much more complex system in place, and used the human system only when it suited them. The Magister's son would no doubt have an important role in the local hierarchy.

"And this explains you not running the brand through normal channels...how?"

"There was a leak in our department — probably more than one. One of the killers was a detective in our unit."

Recalling the details, I cursed under my breath. "Right.

Helping his psycho girlfriend or whatever."

"That's the official version, but I think he had been working for Nicolas Chevalier—the Magister's son—all along. That detective, and others like him, are why Nicolas is able to squirm his way out of charges. If he's infiltrated the local police so effectively, I have to assume that he also has eyes in the agency." He took a deep breath and let it out in a rush. Then moving precisely and slowly, he walked to the couch and sat across from me. His eyes caught mine, and I couldn't look away.

It wasn't just the ice-blue pureness of his irises—although they were striking—it was something else that held me. And for a brief moment, memory flooded back. His strong arms around me. His nimble hands sliding down my body. His wet mouth against my neck.

"I know that if I take this through the normal channels, he'll find out I have the brand. He'll bury this—whatever this is. His latest scheme. And he's got something big going—all the hints and bits of evidence I can find point to something going down soon. Very soon.

"Most of the big things I've connected him to—circumstantially—that he's done lately have occurred while I've been out of town on vampire business. And I'm scheduled again next week on business for Luc. This time for a few weeks, longer than I've been gone for years. Very convenient timing for him. He'll strike then."

I shook myself, and looked away. "You're talking about the son of one of the most powerful vampires in the country."

"Yes. I'm aware of that. But Beatrice, if he pulls off whatever he's working on, it's going to be bad. Something that'll hurt a lot of people. And I don't see him succeeding without taking out some key people first. Like his father."

"What do you think his endgame is?"

"Knowing Nic? Power. He covets his father's position. He might be making a move to take over." He frowned. "But to take over as a local Magister, he'd need local otherworlder support. Leaders of various factions. And he'd have to deal with any challengers among Luc's clan."

"I take it the current Magister would have to have moved on for this plan to work?" Damn. If there was even the slightest chance of a huge upheaval in the local vampire world, it was big. Too big for the two of us to handle. But what were the odds he was right, and that no one had picked up on this big plot except for him?

"Yes. Luc would have to be dead—or have agreed to step down, which isn't likely." His tone took on a fervent quality. "Nic would have to take out his father either in a challenge fight, which will never happen because Luc would wipe the floor with him one-on-one. Or, he'd have to take out Luc without being connected to it."

"Have you ever taken this to the Magister? Sounds like something he'd be equipped to deal with."

Claude's expression turned grim. "I've taken many things concerning Nic to Luc, but he cannot bring himself to admit Nic's nature. For me to prove this to him, the evidence must be ironclad. Undeniable."

"I'll be honest, you sound a little off-kilter. And this is all just a story right now. You said yourself the evidence seems thin." My assessment was too honest. Uncomfortable, I shifted in my seat, keeping my eyes purposefully away from his, though the desire to look into that light blue ocean gripped me. Was this some kind of strange vampire power

I'd never heard of? Or was it just leftover attraction—simple fascination?

Or was I lonely?

Okay, sure, our past might have pushed me to get on that plane to Chicago—but getting more information about the vampire from my dream was the main reason. Any residual feelings were just that—leftover from our past with no bearing on our present.

"This could get you into a lot of trouble," I pointed out.

"It won't."

"You think that you're not breaking any laws by investigating this on your own, off the books?" I couldn't help the derision in my tone.

He turned to face me. My gaze locked with his, and raw emotion flashed in his eyes. What emotion, I couldn't be certain. It was gone before I could get a read on it.

"I'm not breaking any laws. There aren't any bodies that can be tied to this brand—not yet. Once I get that tie, I'll have enough to make a case." His expression turned grim. "But I think that's going to be especially difficult. The brand must have been spelled, somehow, to affect your power."

"Excuse me?" If I'd been a cat, my fur would have bristled. The idea of something affecting my power was ridiculous. "That's impossible. Why the hell would you think that?"

"Because the face you drew—it's not possible he was involved."

"What? Why not?"

"Because he's a friend."

My pride flared at the insinuation that my powers could be corrupted. "Maybe you know him, but I'll bet you anything that you're wrong."

"Anything?" He quirked an eyebrow at me and I felt my face flush. As if my reaction invited him, he leaned into my space. My stomach tensed, but I didn't move back. Not even when he reached up and tucked a bit of hair behind my ear. "Now that's a bet I'd like to lose."

Chapter Three

A couple of hours later, Claude was showing me to his guest room.

We'd just returned from delivering the brand to Natalie, a Covenant witch, who seemed more like a friend than a colleague to Claude. She thought his theory that the brand was spelled to give an inaccurate vision to be far-fetched. But she had promised to look into it — for a fee, of course. Friend of Claude's or no, she was still a Covenant witch.

The vampire guided me down the corridor, confident and a little distracted, as if my staying with him wasn't a big deal. As if he lent the room often. For all I knew, he did.

Staying here made more sense than going to a hotel. And the part of my mind that disagreed could kindly shut the hell up.

But he had a point. If this vampire Nicolas had gone after cops on his trail before, he'd be likely to do it again. I would rest just a little easier with a powerful vampire down the hall. A hotel might not be safe.

"Do you get a lot of visitors?" I asked, once I'd freshened up and met him back in the kitchen. Takeout Indian food lined the countertop, and I climbed onto a bar stool and reached for my Styrofoam container.

"Loads. It's a regular hotel-motel around here," he said from the other side of the breakfast bar. I raised an eyebrow at that and he laughed. "Occasionally. Vampires have friends, you know."

Heat flushed my cheeks. Of course vampires had friends, and after working in the OWEA with all sorts of different otherworlders, I had to admit that most were very similar to humans in how they acted—at least on the surface. But behind closed doors…

Well, I'd seen a lot of weird shit on the job, too.

"So let's talk about it," I said. No point in avoiding the topic any longer. I needed to know who the man in that picture was. That was why I was still here, after all. Helping Claude was purely secondary. And if I continued to repeat that, eventually I'd believe it.

He sipped a dark red wine that lingered on the glass in such a way that it made me wonder. But Claude was private, and didn't strike me as brazen enough to drink blood in front of me without asking.

"Talk about what? The Indian food? Because it smells divine—"

"Drop the bullshit, Claude. Who is the man in the picture?"

"Why is he so important to you?"

Because my vision of the vampire was real, whether Claude believed it or not. More than that, it confirmed the vision I'd had during my childhood—when I should have been too young to have a psychometric vision—had been real, despite everyone's insistence.

And that meant Claude's friend had been involved in more than one murder.

Suddenly the air around me disappeared, and the world twisted. Of course. Few events were traumatic enough to psychically imprint an event on an object.

The same bit of logic followed for that piece of my brother's coat.

My older brother, Eddie—nine years my senior—had almost definitely died before they found part of his jacket. Before I'd touched it. Before the police officer had brought it by for my parents to identify.

The officer had been careless while he comforted my parents and had left it on the table where I, a curious ten-year-old, happened upon it. But how could he have known it would spur a vision that would influence my entire life?

"I'm the one who's taking time out of my life to help you on an investigation that could lead to misconduct charges. I deserve to know what you know," I said.

"Oh, I hardly think your job is at risk—you are far too valuable." He leaned toward me. The breakfast bar kept a safe distance between us, but the slight smell of him—spicy and clean—drifted to me, present even with the Indian food permeating the air. A grin touched his lips, as if he could see my mental squirming and he resumed his perfectly straight posture. "Your powers as a psychometrist are quite important to them."

That I'd been thinking almost the exact same thing irritated me. That I wanted to lean toward him to see if the intoxicating smell of him was real or imagined irritated me even more. "Not the point."

"And what would you be doing if you weren't here, helping? Not working a case, that's for sure." He took a sip of his hopefully-wine as I processed what he'd said. "Not until psych signs off on you."

Embarrassment warred with anger, and they mixed to run through me in a sickening wave. He knew. He knew that I'd been put on a leave of absence. Sure, it was something that happened to psychometrists, and most went back to work afterward for another year or two, until the pressure built back up and they had to decompress again.

Until the dreams and dark thoughts pushed them to a point where they couldn't function in their jobs anymore.

But the idea that Claude knew—a man I'd admired, a man who had probably never shown a moment of weakness in his life—shook me to my core.

Who else knew? Fuck.

I couldn't let him know how much this bothered me. I twisted my finger out of the bit of hair I'd unconsciously wrapped around it, and then slammed my hand down on his counter—making a most unsatisfying low thump. Stupid granite countertops. "Tell me now or I'm out of here."

"I'm sorry," Claude murmured, mouth only inches from my hair.

I jumped. He stood next to me now. Fast would be an understatement.

"I had no right—"

"Whatever." I waved off the hand he was trying to touch my shoulder with. I didn't need comfort. "Just tell me who the fuck the vampire from my vision is."

Claude sighed, almost imperceptibly, then walked at a more human speed back to the other side of the breakfast bar where he'd left his half-drunk glass of wine.

"The man in the drawing is Luc Chevalier."

I grabbed the beer he'd gotten me, which I'd left untouched, and tipped it to my lips. The cold liquid slid down my throat, coating it as I downed half the bottle.

"Are you all right?"

"The Magister." The vampire leader for Illinois, Wisconsin, and Iowa. One of the most powerful vampires in the country. And father to the vampire Claude hunted.

The Magister had been involved in my brother's disappearance, and I'd seen it in my vision. I'd convinced myself that the flash—and accompanying nightmares—I'd gotten off my brother's jacket eighteen years before had been my imagination.

But now I knew it was a vision, because the man—the vampire I'd seen fucking existed.

How had I not known? How had I not seen him on the news? He was the vampire equivalent of a local politician—only more powerful. Maybe because most vampires were notoriously camera shy, and I didn't much care about noncriminal-related news anyway.

"I know him, Beatrice. And I know he wouldn't be involved in this mess. Wouldn't take innocent lives."

"You can't be certain of that."

"I can—"

"How? How can you say that for sure? Because old vampires are terrible at hiding things, right? That's how they survive for so long—excessive honesty?"

"I've been friends with the man for centuries. *Centuries.*

Vampires that old don't just change. And he couldn't have hidden ritualistically killing people or torturing them with branding irons for centuries from me."

I found myself, once again, unable to look away from the pale irises. He cared—really cared—about this friend of his. And the way he spoke, it was as if he needed me to believe in the Magister as well.

I turned to look at my beer bottle, still clutched in my hand. "Sometimes, it's the people closest to us who are able to fool us most easily—or we fool ourselves."

"I'm not saying he's an angel—he's not—but he's also not a sociopath. I'm not an idiot, *mon chou*." Exhaustion suddenly soaked his tone, and he leaned against the counter for support.

A shiver ran up my back at the familiar endearment, but I took a deep breath and ignored it. "I'm not saying you are."

"Do you really think that I could be close to him for so long and not notice that kind of flaw? We can only fool ourselves so much."

I thought about that. After centuries at the vampire's side, could he fail to notice a sociopathic nature? Sounded unlikely. And for that to happen to a man like Claude—an investigator at his very core? Hell, I'd heard he'd served in law enforcement for decades, before vampires were even acknowledged as anything more than old wives' tales.

But I couldn't let the idea go.

I forced myself to study the vampire before me. The longish hair, the AC/DC T-shirt, the light blue eyes, and the strong jawline. The wide shoulders and obvious strength in his arms.

Every instinct in my body told me that he was worthy

of trust. Even our time together—with its abrupt ending—supported the fact that he was an honest man. He'd never made me any promises, no matter what my heart had hoped for. But if I trusted him, then I had to give his friend the benefit of the doubt.

Because if Luc Chevalier proved to be a villain, so too, would Claude.

"All right. I'll give your friend the benefit of the doubt," I said, finally, voice thick. So much for telling him about my brother's and Luc's connection. I definitely wasn't going to share it now.

Tension left him so visibly it was like a waterfall rushing to disappear into the floor beneath him. "Thank you."

"But I'm also not letting you investigate this alone."

His head jerked up and his eyes met mine. I stifled a grin. How often was Claude Desmarais startled? Not often, I would wager.

"Why not?"

My urge to smile faded. Saying that I didn't trust him to bring in a man with whom he'd shared several lifetimes of friendship wouldn't encourage him to let me in. "Like you said, I'm not allowed back on active duty for a couple more weeks, and I'm bored."

To my surprise, he didn't argue that it wasn't safe. He didn't even try a halfhearted attempt. Instead, he nodded. "I'd appreciate your insights, especially if Natalie is able to remove whatever is on the brand that's clouding your vision."

Thank God I'd had years to perfect my poker face, otherwise I don't think I could have kept a convincingly blank expression. "We'll see."

He set his wineglass in the sink and then turned to me;

some of the concern I'd thought I'd seen earlier touched his expression. "No playing hero, and no talking about this to anyone but me. I can protect you, but no reason to add to the risk."

"Don't worry. I'm no hero."

"That's not how I remember you."

"Your memory is faulty."

"Is it?" His voice turned wistful. "It's served me well. Gotten me through many nights alone. My memory, and wondering what might have been."

Something shifted in my chest, pushing into my throat. I'd spent more nights thinking about what-ifs than I'd ever admit, too. I took a drink of my beer to buy myself a moment, but my voice still came out hoarse. "Pondering what-ifs is a waste of time, Claude. The past is what it is. We're all on the paths we've chosen."

"The future is hardly set in stone," he said, but I could barely hear him, his voice was so low.

"It might as well be." I drank the rest of my beer and then muttered a good night and headed back to my room, thoughts reeling. Thinking about the emotion I clearly heard in his voice, when he talked about what might have been, was too dangerous. I forced myself to focus on the here and now. On the case. That Claude didn't even try to discourage me from helping on this case seemed…out of character. Either he was exceedingly confident of his ability to protect me, or he was more worried about catching Nicolas than keeping people safe. Me-shaped people anyway.

Or hell, maybe I just didn't know the vampire as well as I thought I did.

Maybe it was time for me to get out while I still could.

Chapter Four

"This place is messed up, little sister."

A toothpick flashed, in and out of his mouth, and I winced at the sight. I always worried he'd stab his cheek with it, or puncture his lip. I'd managed to do both when I'd tried to copy the habit.

Sunlight reflected off his carrot-colored hair, bright despite the cold. It had to be cold—he was wearing his brown, puffy coat. That coat...

"Not a place for a little girl." He spit the toothpick out and stared out into the street beyond. We sat on the edge of a sidewalk, next to a gutter clogged with trash. The musty scent of it touched my nose.

I knew this corner.

I opened my mouth, but he turned to me and I lost my train of thought. His mouth twisted into a wry grin. "But I guess a little girl is all I got, huh? Figures you'd be my only hope."

"I'm not a little girl," I argued, but my voice came out wrong. Different. Young.

His green eyes, so similar to my own, were bleak, but his voice was flat when he spoke.

"Don't let them take me."

Darkness washed over us, as if the whole world had suddenly dropped away from the sun. Streetlamps filled the shadows with their eerie glow. Tires shrieked.

I closed my eyes against the noise. And when I opened them again, my brother was gone. A torn bit of his coat remained, the edge just touching a small pool of blood.

My breath came fast and panic curdled in my stomach, but I couldn't move. A yelp cut through the silence. I couldn't see who was screaming. Couldn't see anything anymore. But I knew who cried out for help. My brother. *He* had my brother. And he'd get me, too.

He was coming for me now. I knew it. I wouldn't be able to get away. I turned my head.

Familiar features, twisted in hunger. A predator's eyes.

He was here.

Sweat soaked my sheets when I awoke, and my heart raced, trying to beat its way out of my chest. I hadn't dreamed of my brother in years—I saw plenty of fresh, new bad things to keep my subconscious busy on cases without my mind needing to dredge up old nightmares. But now, with one touch of a brand and one vision of Claude's Magister, my brother again took center stage in my nightmares.

Going home wasn't an option any longer. Even if Claude

hadn't been involved, I had to stay on this case.

My brother was right. I was his only hope. Even though it was too late to save him, I could find the man responsible for his death.

And I would.

Claude was gone by the time I'd dragged myself out of the shower and into the kitchen. The vampire had brewed fresh coffee. A short note left on the counter beside it said he'd be back soon, and that I should make myself at home.

Right.

I ate fast, grabbing a muffin I found in a small stack next to the coffeemaker, then I sipped coffee while I searched the Internet. There was almost nothing to go on to locate the brand's markings within the seemingly endless streams of data on the web. I needed to confine my search. I needed to get into the OWEA's database.

I grabbed my cell phone and hit Parker's name on my contact list. Two rings, and a deep voice answered.

"Parker. I need your login info for the database."

"I don't know if—"

"It's fine, Parker. Really. I just need to do some research. Nothing stressful. Promise." I crossed my fingers behind my back.

The new recruit, still in his first year on the job, hesitated for a second longer, then rattled off the information. I thanked him and hung up before he could ask me any questions.

He was a good-enough kid, and a good-enough partner. A lycan in his early twenties. Enthusiastic about his job. A decent investigator. Easily led.

Guilt pressed against the back of my mind, but I ignored

it. Yes, I was using my influence as his senior partner. It was an abuse of power. An abuse of the crush he so obviously had on me. But hell, I wasn't asking for much. Nothing he could get more than a slap on the wrist for sharing.

The OWEA database access wasn't fully enabled from a personal laptop hooked up outside of an OWEA office, but I could access the records I needed—the "Items, Mystical and Magical" database. I searched for branding irons first, but there were dozens of records, far more than I expected. I narrowed down the search further by adding in the term "ritual."

Seventeen items remained. The first four proved to be standard irons, where the designs themselves weren't important to the ritual in which they'd been used—it had been the pain that mattered. The next two twisted my stomach, and made me wish I'd never touched the muffin.

The designs weren't important in those either, but the attackers had used their initials to brand their victims. I continued to click through the branding irons, stomach hardening at each picture, at each description. Finally, after looking at fourteen irons where the brand symbology didn't seem relevant to the actual crime, I hit pay dirt.

The symbol of the brand used to mark a man in Butte, Montana, nearly a decade before wasn't at all similar to the one Claude had had me touch, but the symbol was relevant—scratch that, necessary—for the ritual it was used to complete.

But it was the *why* that got me.

The symbol allowed the woman who branded him to drain him of his energy, like a vampire could do through a blood drain, or a succubus could do with sex. The woman who had branded him simply had to touch the branded flesh with a bit of her blood to activate the magic. A magic she could then activate whenever she wanted from a distance, with a bit more blood and a lot of energy.

My breath caught. A shaman.

But shamans didn't tend to deal in murder. With their connection to living things, killing wouldn't be easy for them. I had a hard time wrapping my brain around the idea of a shaman being involved in this.

The sound of a door clicking shut had me reaching for my sidearm—a weapon I no longer possessed, and wouldn't have again until I was back on official duty.

"Beatrice?" Claude's voice rang out, and my blood pressure dropped.

"In the kitchen," I called back.

"I brought lunch." He held up a bag from a local fast food joint, Wolfy's, and I grinned. For a man who didn't require food to live, he sure knew his local eateries.

"Thanks." I pulled a hot dog out of the bag and eyed Claude, who had already started in on his French fries.

"I didn't realize vampires ate so often. I mean—food-food." Had he eaten so much before and I simply hadn't noticed? No. We'd both been too distracted to eat much then. By the case and by each other. For a moment, it was as if I could feel his hand sliding up my side to caress my breast, his clever tongue slipping into my mouth to tease moans from my lips. My breath caught at the memory.

He bit off the end of his fry, flashing me just a tip of fang. "It doesn't give us sustenance like blood does, but that doesn't mean it doesn't taste good." His eyes twinkled and his mouth turned up in a most distracting grin. "Besides, I've found it makes humans more comfortable if they see me eat when they do."

As if I could forget he was a vampire.

"I guess I can see why. Not really any shame in drinking blood though."

His eyes widened and their color struck me again. The man should not be allowed such lovely eyes. "That's not the typical reaction I get. Humans tend to be…uncomfortable when confronted by the realities of my existence." He hesitated, as if choosing his words carefully. "I mean, it's different—witnessing it during an intimate—"

"There's no shame in it," I plowed on and pretended my embarrassment wasn't obvious on my heated cheeks. I refused to let him finish that sentence. Red hair and the pale skin that accompanied it didn't make hiding emotions easy, but I didn't have to acknowledge it. "I don't see people looking askance at a plant for absorbing energy in a way different from us."

"True. But plants aren't potential predators—not of human prey."

"Touché." The easy conversation warmed me, especially since he didn't try to bring up anything intimate again, and we ate the rest of our food in companionable silence. Swallowing the last of my Coke, I closed my eyes.

The brand, orange and bright and full of malice, filled my sight.

Claude patted my back as I choked, coughing out the soda I'd inhaled.

"Are you all right?" His hand lingered on my back, soft pressure sending warmth into my center and bits of electricity up my spine. And I almost imagined I felt a soft brush of his thumb stroking me before his hand dropped and he walked back around to the kitchen side of the breakfast bar.

"Sorry," I spluttered out from behind the napkin I'd managed to cough most of the soda into. I didn't want to tell him about the vision echo, so I didn't give him a chance to ask. It would only worry him, make him want to send me home. I'd lose any chance at finding out what had happened all those years ago to my brother.

And he'd be trying to take down Nicolas Chevalier alone.

"What do you know about shamans?"

He didn't blink at the sudden change of subject. "As much as the next man who's been around awhile, I guess. Why do you ask?"

"Was there an indication of shamanic magic on the brand? Wherever you actually happened upon it?"

"It's rude to answer a question with a question," he said, but amusement laced his tone.

"Did I ever claim to be polite?" I couldn't help grinning at my jibe.

His smile widened. "Quite right. You win—yes, there was shamanic magic on the brand. Just a touch, but my partner is a sensitive, and quite good at her job."

I ignored the twinge in my chest at his obvious affection for his partner, and the desire to ask him where she was in all this. If they were so close—and she was so good at her job—then why wasn't she here helping? Granted, sensitives didn't get visions from objects like psychometrists did, but they were able to feel the energy exuded by otherworlders— even traces left behind on objects.

Useful was hardly a strong enough word for them.

"So as to what I know of them, shamans are a varied lot," he continued. "They're all spirit-oriented—both human and animal. As a result they tend to be very tied into the energy around them. Empathetic."

"Nature lovers."

He laughed. "That too, I suppose."

"I found something similar to your brand in the OWEA database. Well, similar enough. A brand used in a ritual with shamanic magic involved."

His smile faltered. "I told you—"

"I'm not looking deep enough for anyone to get pinged or even be able to see I was there beyond a standard search. I just hit the general objects database. Of course, if we want more details about the case—"

"Not now. Not yet anyway. Tell me what you found."

Bossy. I frowned at him, but didn't argue. "I don't think it's directly related to what you found, but a brand was used by a woman practicing shamanic magic a decade ago. She branded a symbol into a man's chest and used it to drain him of his energy."

"That sounds unlikely for a shaman."

"I Googled it after. According to news articles, she'd utterly lost it after her child was killed. The branding victim was responsible—DUI."

"How did it work exactly?"

"Not enough detail in the general database file to be able to tell. But it wasn't an overnight thing. She killed him over a period of months."

Claude interlaced his fingers and stretched his shoulders. "Well, guess we may need to risk exposure to get the file."

"Do you really think he might have spies in the OWEA?"

"I think it's possible — hell, probable. Why wouldn't he?"

I opened my mouth to tell him that he was wrong. That the OWEA stood for something, and the people in it were decent, hardworking law enforcement officers who wouldn't sell out. I snapped my mouth shut and gave him a short nod instead.

A wistful smile touched his mouth. "For a second there, you reminded me of someone."

My heart jumped, racing for no reason I could fathom. "Who?"

"A fiery redheaded rookie, who believed that justice would always prevail."

"You're wrong. I was never that naive." Not since I was a little girl who'd lost her older brother. Not since the mystery of what had happened to him had gone unsolved. Not since I'd seen a vision of Luc Chevalier when I was ten years old, a vision everyone had told me was simply a nightmare. "And I'm not fiery."

"If you say so." His joke failed. The wistfulness faded from his expression, and he almost looked a little sad. "But you did have a certain optimism."

Years of visions and nightmares had robbed me of that, but I couldn't say it aloud. "I'm a realist now."

"Not a cynic?" His grin returned, and I couldn't help the tug at my own lips.

"Not yet."

If I'd thought visiting the house of a Covenant witch in the cold Chicago winter irritating, I'd have been wrong. It had nothing on slinking down a dark alley with the wind whipping off Lake Michigan to visit a man the Covenant witch, Natalie, had suggested might have information about the brand. But the wind was the only relief to be found from the stink of old garbage and worse things that inundated the alley. The chill or the stench, I wasn't sure which was worse.

And I wasn't even getting paid to deal with this bullshit.

"Here we are." Claude halted in front of a black door painted in such a flat tone it looked as if it had been done with a spray can.

I bumped elbows with Claude as he knocked and saw what had caught his vampire eyes. A tiny symbol—three lines stacked, evenly spaced, only about an inch long, with an odd swirl beneath them. They appeared to have been scratched into the paint.

"Lovely," I muttered, and the door swung open.

I backed up a step, and with one hand I reached for the gun I no longer carried, and with the other hand I sought a badge that I'd surrendered. The man filled the doorway, a giant who I suspected would have to bend down simply to walk through the space. But he wasn't only tall, his shoulders were wide and he had arms bigger than my head. I'd have thought him a giant, if giants had been real. He dwarfed Claude.

"Yeah?" he said through the long black beard, peppered in gray, that covered his face and neck.

"Customers."

Claude looked as if he would have said more, but the man was no longer listening. After the word *customers,* he jerked his head at us and turned, letting the door fall from his grip. Claude caught it gracefully, as if he'd expected the man to take off. Thank goodness for vampire reflexes.

Claude shot me a reassuring grin and I frowned. I'd needed to be reassured by him at one point in my life—but no longer.

The alleyway had smelled bad, but the inky dark hallway smelled purely frightening. Not stinky—no. But the scents of the alleyway had at least been identifiable—normal, even. The hallway stank of fire and smoke and pain.

No. That was the memory of the vision talking. The smoke that had triggered the memory, yes, that was here, but not the pain. Not the blinding brightness of the enflamed branding iron. I blinked quickly even as I followed Claude closely, suppressing the urge to grip his jacket to make sure I didn't get lost, and pushing down the urge to panic.

Claude didn't seem to have any trouble navigating the hallway, and I silently envied him his vampire sight. We followed the man until the hallway tilted—a ramp leading down into even greater darkness.

My heart jumped into my throat. I didn't speak, didn't cry out, but Claude paused to reach back and take my hand in his. A rush of relief ran through me at the touch and, my resolve wavering, I let him hold my hand. But I managed to suppress my desire to grasp at him desperately.

After what felt like hours, the ramp evened out and a small room was revealed. Ventilation fans hovered over what looked like old-fashioned blacksmith fire pits, a curious mix of new and old. The fires weren't lit. Instead, a single fluorescent bulb glowed uncovered above a large metal desk that seemed to divide the customer area from the fire pits in the back.

I assumed it was a desk. By the height, it was more accurately described as a counter. But when the big man sat behind it and pulled out a yellow, legal-sized notepad and pen, there was no doubt how he used the thing.

"What're you want'n?" he asked, and I struggled to figure out the accent. Sounded Irish, but was a little off. Maybe he'd lived in the States long enough for it to change a bit. That didn't sound quite right either. But I was no accent expert.

"Information," Claude said.

The giant set the pen down on the notebook and leaned back in his oversized chair. Just as large as he'd appeared outside, he looked even more intimidating under the too-white glow of the fluorescent bulb. Thick gray hair stood at haphazard angles on his head, as if we'd woken him up in the middle of the night. Craggy skin covered the rest of his hide and the backs of his hands. Not pockmarked, but uneven and odd. Burned, I thought. I glanced at the fire pit behind him, and was rewarded with a scowl.

"Ain't got no information for the likes of you."

"What's the matter? Don't like cops?" Claude slapped his badge down on the counter.

The giant leaned back, crossing his big arms across his chest. "Don't like fangers."

Claude went still—too still—like only vampires could. "I don't much care if you like me," he said, voice still even, almost amused. "I'll bet you don't care either. When it comes down to it, my money spends just as well as the next guy's."

The beard moved, revealing yellowed teeth set in a frightening smile. "S'pose it does, at that."

Claude pulled out my drawing of the brand and set it on

the man's desk. "I need to know everything you know about this symbol."

The man named a figure that made me gasp.

"You're ripping me off!" Claude jabbed his finger at the giant.

I gaped; I'd never seen the vampire yell.

"Damn right, I am! That'll teach ya not to be so cocky." An evil glint touched his narrowed eyes. "Maybe should charge ya double."

"Maybe I should kick the piss out of your witch ass."

"Like to see you try, shrimp."

"Oaf!"

Their insults grew cruder and more extravagant, and amusement broke slowly onto both of their expressions as my mood darkened. They were friends and he'd let me assume we might be in danger. Not funny.

After Claude suggested something wholly anatomically unlikely, the witch laughed, and the booming sound filled all the corners of the room. He named another price, about half the original one he'd suggested. It was still astronomical by my scale.

Claude grinned, but didn't hesitate in his reply. "Done."

"But that's—"

"It's fine," Claude said, shooting me a wink.

Whatever. It was his money. What did I care that it was more than I made in half a year?

"I'll call you when I have somethin' for ya, if there's somethin' to be found."

I made an exasperated noise, and Claude glanced at me.

"How do you know you can trust him?" I asked him.

"I'll be back in two days, whether you've called or not.

I would like to have it in my possession before the gala," Claude told the giant, ignoring my question.

"What gala?" I asked.

Finally Claude's attention shifted to me, but before he could answer the giant spoke.

"There's a fancy vampire bash this weekend. Goin' to be borin' as all get out, but a fanger'll take any chance to put on a shiny suit, eh?"

Claude shot the giant a glare before turning back to me. "The Chevaliers throw a gala event for the local other-worlder elite every few months."

"Tryin' to remind people they think they're in charge," the giant grumbled.

Claude waved a hand. "It's not important, but this brand and my timeline are. Two days."

"Fine," the man said. "Two days. But I'm gonna need some specifics from ya, about the metal and such. Can't make nothin' worth workin' powerful magic with that ain't made right. The metal—it'll tell us somethin'."

Claude nodded and set an envelope on the counter, no doubt the down payment for services that by my guess might not ever get done. We turned to go, but the giant's words followed us down his endless hallway.

"Damn fanger."

Chapter Five

"I can't believe you paid a man—probably a criminal—that kind of money. And for what? Probably nothing," I groused after Claude called Natalie and instructed her to send the details of the brand's metal composition to the giant—how the witch would determine that, I had no idea. A spell? A home chemistry kit? Claude handed over some of the takeout he had again picked up. "Not to mention that show of insults. I take it you know each other?"

Of course they did, and probably well. And Claude hadn't bothered to warn me about their weird, macho idea of friendship. I'd been convinced I'd have to run from a fight. Dammit. I needed my sidearm. At least it gave me the illusion of being on even ground.

"Judging people based on looks alone? Beneath you, *mon chou*, to stereotype. You don't know for sure he's a criminal." The vampire was annoyingly unflappable, and he munched on his orange chicken like he didn't have a care in the world.

I blinked. "Isn't he?"

Claude's grin widened. "Oh, yes. He's quite the criminal. But that doesn't mean you should stereotype."

Ass.

"But minor things, nothing violent. Do you have a better idea than paying off my criminal friend?"

"As a matter of fact, yes. I do have a better idea. We could pull in your partner. A sensitive could probably help a ton. Hell, she could have helped us at that giant's. She could've probably sensed out a dozen reasons for us to have arrested him, or avoided paying him for nothing."

A flash of pain touched his expression. "Astrid is still recovering from injuries from the Chevalier's casino ship case."

I started at that. A month had passed since that case. She had to have been hurt worse than I'd thought. "I'm sorry. I didn't realize she'd been so badly injured."

"It could have been much worse. But I don't particularly want to drag her into something new, even if she was at 100 percent. It takes a while to fully recover from something like that—more than just healing from physical wounds. If we get something that we need a sensitive for, I'll consider it. But not unless we have something solid for her to check out."

I suppressed the urge to yank on my hair out of pure frustration. "Let's pull the OWEA file, then—in full."

"Pulling the file will leave a trace. A trace that'll lead right to your door."

The file would lead right to Parker's door, more likely, since I still didn't have clearance. Or right to my supervisor's door, because Bill would probably pull it for me if I asked. "Well, it's a damn sight more likely to lead us somewhere — unlike paying off your giant friend. And how likely is it that someone would be looking for that exact file to be pulled?"

"It's not unlikely. You said yourself there were few cases similar to this one. If he has someone in the OWEA, he'll be looking to monitor similar cases."

The smell of the food finally overwhelmed my determination to ignore it until this was settled. I grabbed the chicken fried rice and scooped some onto the plate Claude had set out for me. A thought hit me as I reached for the beef and broccoli, and I stopped, my hunger suddenly less important. "Claude, does this guy know his brand is missing?"

"No."

"How can you be sure?"

He took a bite of chicken — to buy himself time, no doubt.

"Look, did you actually just happen upon this somewhere? Or will he have reason to think someone took it? Will he suspect you?" Questions ran through my head faster than I could verbalize them. If this vampire — one who was obviously powerful and strong if he'd evaded Claude for who-knew-how-long — realized that someone was collecting evidence against him, it wouldn't take him long to figure out who. And that put both Claude and me in danger.

He ran a hand through his hair, arm muscles pressing against the confines of his T-shirt. "Nicolas owns a cabin in Wisconsin — technically it's owned by a dead acquaintance of his, to keep anyone from connecting it to him, I'm sure. It's very isolated."

"How did you find out about it?"

He grinned wryly. "The old-fashioned way: police work. Research. Talking to people on the ground, looking through old records."

"Go on."

"I went there when I knew Nic would be out of state. I brought my partner, Astrid, with me. She said the place had been cleaned—psychically. And the only thing she could sense anything on was the brand. It had been stuck in a bin with the fireplace tools."

Shit. This was starting to feel a lot riskier to my job than I'd thought. "You broke in? Stole it?"

His eyes met mine, and my chest tightened. Why did he still have such an effect on me? We hadn't been anything to each other in years—even if we had only been casual lovers enjoying each other's company then.

"Yes."

"And you don't think that he's going to catch on? What the hell, Claude?" I stepped down from the barstool, half wishing I could walk out the door. But I couldn't. Not with the man connected to my brother's disappearance involved.

My prospects weren't good, however. Claude might be able to defend himself from a vampire like Nicolas Chevalier, but I wasn't ignorant enough to think I could. I still wasn't sure that digging into anything related to my brother's disappearance was a good idea. I'd avoided it for years, with good reason.

But some obsessions were harder to shut down than others, and it wasn't a wound I could poke at without consequences.

"Nic hasn't returned to the cabin since we were there, and he's not likely to anytime soon."

"Why do you think that?"

"Because he hadn't been there in six months before I went there. Besides, I have a…friend keeping an eye out. If Nicolas sets foot near that cabin, I'll know about it before he becomes a threat."

Who did he have watching the cabin? And how? The questions were on the tip of my tongue, but I shook my head. No. I didn't need to know any of that, and didn't really want to know.

"I can't imagine why you'd be willing to take a risk not only to your person, but to your career if anyone finds out— but not be willing to pull a damn file," I grumbled.

He let out a short laugh, but there was no humor in the sound. "You really think I'm worried about my career?" He leaned forward, again catching my gaze with his, and my stomach clenched. "I have had many *careers* in my lifetime. I will continue to do what I do, bringing otherworlders and humans to justice for their crimes, whether or not the Chicago Police Department continues to pay me."

"Well, not all of us have the benefit of multiple lifetimes, Claude. Astrid doesn't. I certainly don't."

"I've got it under control. No one's career is at stake, Beatrice."

"From where I'm standing, you have nothing under control. You're not even willing to investigate this the right way, yet you're willing to steal a suspect's property?"

"I suppose you could do better?"

"Damn right I could. I'd start by getting Natalie off that wild goose chase you've got her on, and use her skills on something important instead. Then I'd pull some damn files from the OWEA or the local police Paranormal Unit that are similar. Track down witnesses. Talk to some shamans. See what you can find using real police work."

I got up close and personal, leaving only inches between us. "And I'd take a serious look at your supposed *friend*, Luc Chevalier. Because he isn't clean in all this. I'd bet my life on it."

"I'm telling you that Luc has nothing to do with this," Claude said, his voice a low growl. He stood over me, as if his height would intimidate me. I'd finally rattled the unrattlable vampire. *Go me.*

"And I'm telling you that I don't buy it."

Claude slammed a hand down on his countertop, and the loud boom startled me. He was a better slammer than I was, I'd give him that.

"I need some air," he muttered. Without another word, he turned and walked to the living room. The open floor plan made his destination obvious, and he walked out onto the balcony. Annoyingly, he moved calmly, as if he hadn't just lost his temper.

I struggled with the urge to follow him and continue our argument. Claude might not be able to see it, but he was blinded by his feelings for his friend. And could I blame him?

Minutes turned into nearly an hour, and I finally couldn't leave it alone anymore. I threw on my coat, cursing under my breath. Then I opened the door to the balcony, and stared out at the view. It was lovely. All that dark water — I wouldn't have known it from the ocean. And I wouldn't have even seen it if not for the moon blazing above us. Lights shone below us and to the sides, too, but all man-made. Brisk air filled my lungs, and I was thankful I'd remembered the jacket.

Movement caught my eye. I turned to face Claude. He sat in the corner, a bottle of whiskey on the small table at his side. I suppressed the urge to sigh, knowing my words would land on deaf ears even before I said them. "If it looks like a duck—"

"I get it." Weariness coated his tone.

"I've seen him in another vision, Claude."

"I figured as much, the way you look at the picture you drew. But you don't trust me enough to give me any details about it." It wasn't a question, but I answered anyway.

"It's not about trust."

"I'm sick to death of talking about this. Let's speak of something more pleasant."

I laughed. The situation was just too ridiculous. "You're drunk."

"Nonsense. Vampires don't get drunk."

"Bullshit."

"Why didn't you ever call me back?"

The change of topic spun me, and I couldn't grasp my thoughts. "What?" I managed.

"We had amazing sex for several weeks. I know that I didn't treat you well after, but I called you after the case ended. You never called me back." He spoke slowly, as if talking too fast would be more than I could comprehend.

My mind warred. Half of me wanted to turn around and run into the condo as fast as I could. Avoid this conversation. Avoid this man who inevitably got under my skin.

But my other half was pissed.

"You called me *months* after the case ended, Claude. Three months. And after the way you talked to me, you expected me to be waiting for your call?" I shook my head.

"You were right. It was an affair. Fun. But that's all it was."

His voice was low, but it carried to my ears. "It took me three months to realize I didn't want just an affair with you."

"Well, it took me less than three months to realize an affair was all I wanted."

"I'm sorry for what I said—"

"What part?" I asked. He hesitated, and rage bubbled up inside of me. As did the all too clear memory of exactly what he'd said to me during our final hour together. "Maybe you regret telling me what we had was fun, but it didn't mean anything. That we'd experienced an amusing dalliance you'd grown bored of."

"Beatrice—"

"Your tone was the worst, you know." I hated the catch in my throat, the too-high pitch in my quavering voice. "The disinterested, holier than thou tone that made me feel like a piece of trash. Like a silly little girl who you had to explain the ways of the world to." I shook my head. "For a while I believed you. I thought I was the one in the wrong for telling you that I loved you. I put myself out there—confessed my feelings. That's not something that comes easily for me. And you humiliated me."

The fire drained from his expression, and for a moment I felt like I'd won, as if winning this argument meant a thing.

"I was trying to protect you, for what it's worth."

"Protect me? From what?"

"From my enemies for one—I have acquired a few through the decades." A ghost of a grin touched his mouth. "But most of all, I wanted to protect you from me. From me hurting you even more later on."

"You certainly accomplished that. You can't hurt me

anymore." My mind screamed that was a lie, but I ignored it.

"Can't I?"

"No. You have to care about someone before they can hurt you," I said.

He flinched. The motion should have sent a rush of satisfaction through me, instead it pushed a lump into my throat.

"Then why do I feel like you're more of a threat to me than Nicolas?" he murmured.

There was no way to answer that. This conversation was so over. I turned to leave.

He moved again and stood in front of me before I could face the door to the condo. "You have to admit it was a hell of a few weeks."

You don't have to admit anything, my mind insisted, but panic pushed at my throat. His lips were only inches from mine, and they curled into his familiar flirtatious grin. Darling me.

If I ran away now, it would be as good as admitting I cared. That I hadn't forgotten about our time together. That I hadn't been able to move on, and instead had compared every man I met to him.

And I'd be damned if I admitted anything.

I tilted my chin, ever so slightly. Our lips even closer, I murmured, "I've had better weeks."

A surprised laugh left him, and then his mouth was on mine. His lips were the perfect blend of soft skin and firm demand. It wasn't a first kiss—not even like our first kiss, which had been soft and smooth, testing and wanting. This kiss demanded.

And I responded in kind. Because damn him, he owed

me.

I wrapped my arms around his neck and pulled him closer.

His desire pressed against my stomach, and I could feel the last bit of control I possessed slipping away. His body was hard where I was soft, and slightly cooler than my own. But against the cold night air he felt warm.

A moan escaped me and he pulled me closer.

I jerked away and turned my head because there was no room for me to step back. He tried to reclaim my mouth, and I almost let him. Desire burned through me. I knew the pleasure that waited for me in his arms. I knew the blissful quiet it would bring to my mind as he filled my thoughts, leaving no room for anything else. And I knew that for a time, I could find peace.

But it would be an illusion.

"No."

He stilled, not moving or breathing.

"No?" he asked. And I noticed with no little satisfaction that his voice was rough with the same passion that overwhelmed me.

"We're not doing this," I said with a firmness I didn't really feel.

An ache filled me when he stepped back. The bitter night air felt colder than it had before.

"All right."

Disappointment warred with relief when he didn't ask me why, when he didn't even attempt to convince me. But Claude wasn't the kind of man who convinced women. He probably had to fight them off with a stick.

There didn't seem to be anything else to say. Nothing

that wouldn't either drag us back into an argument about his friend, or open the door to talk about us—and that was a door I wasn't going to open. I couldn't risk being hurt like that again.

So without another word I went back into the apartment, leaving the vampire out in the cold.

Chapter Six

I tossed and turned through the night. Normal for me, but instead of visions of murder running through my mind, thoughts of Claude plagued me.

I'd considered leaving. I'd gone so far as to pull out my bag. But I couldn't leave this case half finished. I couldn't leave a potential tie to my brother's disappearance unchecked. And the idea of leaving Claude alone to face some vampire with the kind of connections the Magister's son had, pushed panic into my throat.

Six years had passed since I'd partnered with the vampire. The case we'd worked had been my first as a full-fledged agent. A rookie, I'd been full of energy, unaffected by nightmares, and enamored of the legendary vampire, Claude Desmarais.

The affair—and that's all it had been—had lasted through the case. Six weeks. And then they had ended. The case and the affair.

And it had ended so badly, I still felt burned.

The way he'd talked to me after I'd confessed that I loved him had made me feel like the lowest of the low. Wrapped in a sheet, I couldn't have felt more naked, more exposed. But I'd already thought of him as a safe harbor. He'd never judged me, never said a harsh word to me. And in the nights we'd been together I'd shared so much with him. My hopes. My history. My fears.

It was only later that I realized he'd never really done the same.

I'd held out hope for a few weeks. Hope that Claude would apologize. I'd dreamed of him confessing that he hadn't meant what he said. That he was sorry. That he'd only said it all in some misguided attempt to keep me safe. Weeks had turned into months, and my warm feelings faded and twisted into hurt and anger. By the time he had called—three months after we'd said our good-byes—I was no longer interested in his apologies.

Now he'd said many of the things I would have given anything to hear back then. But it was too late. Time passing might change little to vampires, but it changed a hell of a lot for me.

When the gray light of dawn peeked in through my window, I finally admitted defeat and dragged myself out of bed and into the shower. Claude was up and on his laptop by the time I got out to the kitchen. I could feel his eyes follow me, and I poured a cup of coffee while I gathered my thoughts.

"I'm not leaving yet."

"I'm glad to hear it," he said.

"That doesn't mean we'll be doing any more kissing." If I could call such an overwhelming moment of passion by such a simple word. "We're professionals."

"I will treat you as such." The intensity in his eyes made my pulse jump and my mouth go dry. "But don't expect last night to be our final chat about us. I don't have a lot of regrets—I try to live true to myself. But I do regret dismissing our time together as an affair. I regret speaking to you cruelly. And those are regrets I intend to remedy."

I gaped at him for several seconds, then turned away. I couldn't allow myself to hope. To think about what could have been. I could too easily see myself fitting into his life, fitting him into mine. Laughing with him in the evenings, talking cases with him during the days. Thinking about what might have been was easy. It just hurt too damn much when it turned into nothing.

"Some things can't be fixed, Claude." I didn't turn to see his reaction. Instead I focused very intently on my coffee. Silence settled over us, awkward and uncomfortable. And when he finally spoke, I turned to face him.

"Natalie called. She's finished with her spells, wants us to come to her house this morning."

"All right, then."

"Beatrice—"

"Let's just get this case solved, Claude." *And for the love of God, not talk about us.* I didn't say it, but surely he could hear the message loud and clear in my voice.

"I just wanted to say thank you. For helping me with this. And that I'll try to be more open-minded."

He'd try to consider his friend a suspect. That's what he

meant. As far as commitments went, it wasn't the best. But it was a step in the right direction.

"Let's go see your witch."

The drive to Natalie's went far too quickly, and her home looked no less imposing in the light of day.

Claude let us in this time, not even bothering to knock, and I couldn't help wondering again how close he was to this witch.

"Where exactly are we going?" I asked, following Claude down a long hallway. We emerged in what felt like another building. More of the cold winter had penetrated this area than the main living space we'd been in before. We passed a small bathroom, door wide open, then what looked like Chicago's version of a sunroom. All windows and outdoor furniture and sliding glass doors.

We finally had nowhere else to go, but at the end of the hallway stood a set of double doors. The wood was old and thick. Were we headed back outside?

Claude knocked loudly, and a muffled noise came from beyond the doors. I couldn't make out the words, but the vampire apparently could because he opened the doors. They didn't lead outside. On the contrary, they led to a casting room.

I'd seen witches' casting rooms before, but those had mostly been the circles of wannabe witches. Amateurs.

I'd never seen anything like this.

Natalie's was quite big, for one thing—several hundred square feet. A large circle occupied much of the space, and it had been carved into the floor—a floor that looked like it was made of natural stone.

Aside from the circle, a small table was built into one

of the walls, and upon it sat a few tools and bowls, likely for mixing spell ingredients.

"Welcome," Natalie said, dryly. "Couldn't wait in the living room for me, could you?"

I felt heat rising up my neck, even though I wasn't responsible for our presence here.

"Patience is not among my virtues," Claude replied in the same tone.

For some reason, their good-natured ribbing made me almost as uncomfortable as being in a Covenant witch's casting room without her permission or invitation.

"This is quite a casting room," I said.

A small smile crept onto her mouth, and she gave up her attempt to appear angry with Claude.

"Thank you. It's taken me a while to build it." She walked to the table, grabbed the brand from behind a bowl, and flashed it at us. "Let's continue this discussion in the living room, shall we?"

We followed Natalie to the kitchen, a large room that was cut off from the rest of the living space, to pick up tea on our way to the living room. I distracted myself by looking at her crown moldings in an effort not to say something rude, like hurry up and tell us already. Claude revealed no impatience in his laid-back attitude and easy smile.

His attitude changed the second Natalie told us her findings.

"What do you mean, nothing?" he asked, voice strained.

"Nothing to indicate the brand was psychically altered, other than the cleaning, which as you know didn't remove the psychometric imprints. At least not completely," Natalie said, the diminutive woman not the least bit rattled by Claude's obvious shock.

Claude sank onto Natalie's couch and rubbed his face with his hands. "That isn't possible."

I'd never thought I'd hear a man like Claude Desmarais with desperation on his tongue, even just a hint, and I didn't like it. "There could be an explanation, Claude."

He looked up at me and the hope in his gaze twisted my heart.

"I'm not saying that it's likely—his face coming up in the initial vision means he definitely made an impression on the victim. But we don't know exactly what happened. I need more time with the brand." I glanced at Natalie and she offered me a small smile. "I could even start now."

Natalie set down the brand on the coffee table. "I'll just get us some drinks, then. Dealing with murders is a bit easier with alcohol. Scotch for you, Claude?"

He nodded without looking at her, his attention locked on the brand.

"Agent Davis?"

I opened my mouth to tell her I'd take a soda, but changed my mind. If I was going to handle that brand before we left, I'd need a drink after. "Beer if you have it." Hell, what time was it? Noon, maybe? My psychologist would love this—it would open up a whole new can of worms.

"Remember to keep an open mind?" I didn't mean for it to be a question, but my tone lilted anyway. I wanted to go and give Claude a hug, a kiss, offer him comfort. God, I was a world-class masochist.

He nodded, offering me a grateful smile. I sat on one of

the oversized chairs that surrounded the coffee table and hyperventilated. Then I gestured toward the brand. Claude picked it up and held it out to me.

"Thank you," he said softly, then dropped the brand into my outstretched hand.

Fear rolled over me, filling my throat with bile. Luc Chevalier's face flashed, and it intermingled with the branding iron in a most disturbing way. He was yelling something—silent to my ears—and another man came into view. The background was clouded, but I thought I could make out earth beneath my feet. I tore my gaze away, trying to drag it back to the men. But it caught on my arm. On my hand.

On my webbed fingers and graying hand. No, not graying. But touched with fur.

I heard the bang of the brand hitting the floor, and I forced air into my lungs. I blinked away the black spots that pinged my vision. My hand came into focus first, curled like a claw forced open. A defense mechanism that psychometrists' bodies seemed to act out instinctually. One that kept us from recycling through visions, in case we couldn't muster the wherewithal to drop the object during the brief moments between images.

My hand, what was it about my hand?

The vision rushed back, bits and pieces that made no sense. My mind struggled to force them into a linear time line, into some kind of order. A square peg and a round hole, unfortunately.

Someone gripped my arm; I could feel that much again. And I blinked dumbly at Claude for a couple of seconds. The situation rushed back to me and I pulled away, averting my eyes from the strangely concerned expression on his face.

Natalie set a beer on the table in front of me and then reached down and retrieved the brand from where I'd dropped it on her floor. I wondered if she'd seen me. Psychometry visions weren't pretty things, although I mostly sat stiffly without breathing, or so I was told. And I guessed that wasn't so bad.

"A selkie."

"What?" Claude hadn't moved from where he kneeled next to me, although he kept his hands to himself since I'd pulled away.

"The man who imprinted on that brand. He was a selkie. I saw his hand tied down." I touched my own hand, my mind still half expecting to see it changing from a human to a seal. "Webbed fingers—fur just peeking through."

"He was kept in mid-transformation?" Natalie asked.

I shook my head, then regretted the motion as pain shot through my skull. "Not necessarily. Imprints aren't linear, and they aren't perfect. It could be that he shifted entirely, but that the psychic imprint happened during the shift."

"Wow. How do you ever figure out anything useful from your visions?" Natalie asked.

I flinched.

"Apparently she does just fine, Natalie. Have you seen her closure rate?" Claude cut in.

I stared at the vampire. He hadn't just come to me because of my reputation and our history—he'd done some serious digging beforehand. Not that it wasn't a reasonable step—a smart move, for an investigator. No wonder he'd known I was on medical leave.

The small part of me that hoped he'd come because he'd felt a connection to me withered.

And despite my anger at myself for even entertaining such an idea, it was disappointing.

Natalie looked embarrassed, and she shouldn't have. Sure, her comment wasn't tactful, but she hadn't intended any harm. Hell, I was surprised myself when I was able to get a particularly confusing vision to make sense eventually.

"It's okay. Don't worry about it," I said to Natalie. I couldn't deal with Claude right now. Our kiss was too fresh, and it tugged on very old wounds that I didn't have the strength or the gumption to open right now. "Truth is, psychometrists don't always find useful evidence from visions, and we can't always make sense of them." I picked up the beer and took a long drink, then coughed a little. The dark beer was a little stronger than what I normally drank. "Like the vamp said, I usually do come up with something helpful. But not with just one vision. Or two. Usually, it takes a week or two of consistent visions to make any sense out of them."

"That sounds…unpleasant."

I forced a smile. "It's fine."

Natalie still seemed embarrassed, but she also seemed as intent to forget it as I was. "So where does this leave you?" she asked Claude.

The heat of his gaze hit me for a brief moment, then his eyes were back on Natalie. "I've been told I need to be more open-minded. I suppose an open-minded person might start digging through police files."

I took another drink of the beer to hide my smile from the vampire and the witch.

"You gave me selkie with 'man hands.' There are only two adult male selkies who have disappeared in the last fifteen years in the area. The most recent was investigated by the succubus, Marisol. Talking to her is safer than digging through the file. Requesting it will leave a trace."

"Yadda yadda. I got it. No trace, no one putting two and two together." We walked between the short granite columns that protected the building from car bombs and angry drivers. I blew a puff of warm air into my hands. So damn cold.

We walked through the revolving doors into the courthouse, pausing briefly to get through security, before cutting through the marble-lined halls to make our way to the cafeteria. I was already uncomfortable and we hadn't even seen her yet. "Are you sure we should be bothering her?"

"Marisol's in court all week for a case. She has to eat, right?"

Claude cut through the crowd to a small table in the back. The succubus took my breath away. Succubi had that effect on people. That I suddenly felt like a jerk wasn't succubus related.

I had never made such an ass of myself as I had toward Marisol Whitman. Granted, she'd forgiven me after I'd been a total bitch when I found her and my ex-partner in bed together, but I still felt like an ass every time I saw her. But she was a good cop, and my bad behavior in the past and discomfort in the present wasn't good enough reason to avoid talking to her about this case.

Claude pulled out the chair next to me, directly across from Marisol.

"You sounded so mysterious on the phone." Marisol

leaned back in her chair and crossed her arms.

"I have to sound mysterious. How will I keep my reputation intact if I don't?" Claude smiled, but worry prevented his eyes from following suit. "I just have some questions about an old case you were on. Might be nothing, but I need to keep this between the three of us for now."

Marisol frowned. "All right. What case?"

"A selkie disappeared last year, a man named Lawrence Coates."

"Oh, yes. I remember the case. Took two days for the family to even tell us he was a selkie. Case was turned over to the PNU then."

"What else can you tell us about it?"

She shrugged, perfect shoulders sliding under her long, blond hair. "Not much to tell. Not a local, but had some business in the area. His wife called it in when he never went back to their hotel after a dinner meeting. He was some kind of big player in selkie politics. That's why they were so concerned about letting his otherworlder status out."

I started. "I didn't even realize selkies were organized enough for politics."

"You and me both. But there are a lot of them, so I guess it makes sense. We just don't see them much here since we're so far from the ocean."

"Selkies have very little hierarchy," Claude said. "Only the royal family is considered above the others. You must have had some sort of selkie prince on your hands."

"Wait, what? Selkies have a royal family?"

I was glad that Marisol voiced the question, so I didn't have to. I'd never heard of such a thing.

"It's not common knowledge." Claude grimaced. "It's

not even uncommon knowledge, and the selkies would prefer to keep it that way, if you don't mind."

"How do you—" I started at the same time as Marisol said, "Is that even possible?"

He glanced at me. "I saved a selkie royal from a rogue vamp a while back." He turned back to Marisol. "It is possible. So tell us the rest. Did you ever figure out what happened to him? Did you ever find a body?"

It was Marisol's turn to look startled. "A body? No. He didn't die. He showed up a week later—really pissed off that we were looking for him."

I suppressed a sigh. A selkie who hadn't actually disappeared. What a waste of time.

"Well, thanks for taking the time to talk to us," I said, then stopped as Claude held up his hand.

"Give us a rundown."

I shot him the stink eye. Seriously?

"All right," Marisol said, as she leaned back in her chair and tapped her chin. "Wife called the cops in the middle of the first night when he hadn't shown up after a dinner meeting. They explained that he wasn't technically missing yet. At some point—the next morning, I think—she showed up at the station, demanding help. Duty cop took pity on her and let her talk to a detective. They started on the investigation unofficially after that. It became official after he'd been gone long enough."

"How long was he gone before he came back?" Claude asked.

"A week."

"And his explanation for taking off like that?"

"He didn't really give one. And honestly, as an adult, he

can take off on his wife if he really wants to. Nothing illegal about that."

"You think he was stepping out on her? That's where he was that week?" I cut in. If that was the case, this trip really had been a waste of time.

"Can't say for sure, although he insinuated as much the second his wife left the room. But…" She shook her head.

"What is it?" Claude leaned forward, a hunter scenting prey. He knew when blood hit the water.

"Well, it was just a gut feeling, but something was off about how he answered our questions. Like he really didn't want us to ask about that week, and was angry about the whole thing. And he just seemed a little…"

"What?"

"Off, I guess. Sorry I can't be more specific, but he shut us down pretty quickly." She brushed her long hair back from her face.

Claude grimaced again and leaned back on his chair.

"I wish I could tell you more, but the man was an adult. We had no crime to hold him for. No reason to continue questioning him after he was done talking to us."

"Well, thanks for the info." Claude stood. "We'll let you eat your lunch."

We headed out of the cafeteria and Claude had his cell phone in hand before we hit the parking lot, running down the selkie's name with who knew what kind of shady contact.

"Want to go for a drive?" he asked without preamble after shoving his cell phone back in his pocket. He didn't wait for my reply. "Lawrence Coates is in Milwaukee right now. Let's go talk to that selkie about where the hell he was during that missing week."

Chapter Seven

"You seemed tense around Marisol." We'd made it out of the northernmost burbs before he asked. Just long enough of a drive for me to relax.

I acted like a jerk to her a while back, one of my more *brilliant* moments in life. It's not a big deal."

"You're too tense for it not to be a big deal."

"You've gone through my file. I'm sure you know that my ex-partner is now living here, with her." Admitting to Claude how I'd acted was almost as uncomfortable as talking to Marisol. "He was still my partner when they started dating, and I didn't handle it well. I acted like a jealous girlfriend."

He shrugged, tips of his longish hair brushing his collar. "I just…"

"What?" Irritation flared inside of me. Between the case and Claude's kiss and having to see Marisol, I was running on a short fuse. Why'd the man have to poke at all of my sore spots during the same week?

"Did you have feelings for him — her boyfriend, your ex-partner? I mean, were you two involved?" His expression had hardened, and the skin around his eyes crinkled as if he cared about my answer.

"Yes. And no."

His hands tightened on the steering wheel. "What's that supposed to mean?"

"I can't believe we're having this conversation." I rubbed my face with my hands. "Not that it's any of your business, but yes, I have feelings for my ex-partner." I could see his grip tighten even more. Pretty soon the damn steering wheel would bend. "Not romantic feelings, if that's what you're getting at. Friend feelings. Partner feelings."

His grip loosened and he stroked the wheel as if apologizing silently for assaulting it. "So you weren't involved with him."

"No. I was never involved with him. I was just really rude to Marisol once, and I still feel like a jerk every time I'm around her," I grumbled.

A smile touched his lips and he reached for the stereo's volume. "Good."

I stared at him, but before I could form a reply to that, he turned up the volume and an old Journey song filled the air. Fine. Whatever. I didn't want to explore why he thought that was good.

"That doesn't mean I'm interested in anything other than working with you on this case," I said loudly.

He gave me a striking grin, his eyes merry and full of confidence. "I'll just have to convince you."

My breath caught and I turned to watch the snow-covered ground fly by outside my window. I didn't have a good response for that, and was determined he wouldn't see the blush he'd caused.

After ten minutes or so of awkward silence, we passed the rest of the trip to Milwaukee with idle chatter. Claude acted happy enough to talk about unimportant subjects, but his mind seemed to be on other things. As was mine. I tried to push down the antsy feeling that always hit me when I entered this city. I wasn't going to my parents' house. No one was going to lecture me for days, urging me to quit my job. I needed to keep my mind on the case.

How long could I let this investigation go on without pushing to interview Luc? Without pushing Claude to acknowledge that his friend was dirty?

I glanced at the vampire. His concentration was now focused on locating the right address down the winding road outside of Wisconsin's beer destination. Worry creased his mouth, but he had the same strong jawline as I remembered. The same shining hair and the same full lips.

I wondered if I looked the same to him, or if he saw the subtle way the years had touched my skin.

Not that it mattered.

Claude parked the car in front of a sprawling two-story, more mansion than house. With a circular drive, small windows revealing the second story, and marble columns around the front door, the Georgian style wasn't to my personal taste, but it was pretty. And the place probably cost more than I'd make in my lifetime.

"Is he expecting us?"

Claude grinned. "Nope."

The woman who answered the door didn't seem surprised to see us, until Claude flashed his badge and asked to see Lawrence Coates. I couldn't read her physically like Claude could, but there was a certain wariness around her eyes when she stepped back to allow us entry.

The woman, who introduced herself as Joan Coates, Lawrence's sister, led us to a bright sitting room decorated in furniture far too garish for my taste. French or some other older European style, I guessed. Wood covered all the walls, and the red and blue rug clashed with the green and yellow floral furniture. I guessed there was a little green in the rug, but still. Looking at all the busy patterns made me dizzy.

She called for her brother. After offering us tea, which we refused, she excused herself—to go to the market, or so she said. I suspected she just wanted to get away from us. And perhaps especially Claude. He was a touch pale, but he moved like a human when he wanted to appear to be one. His fear aura couldn't be triggering her response since his was so subtle.

But perhaps selkies could sense what he was. I knew less about the notoriously shy ocean-goers than I should have. They simply didn't come up in OWEA investigations as often as vampires and other more aggressive otherworlders.

"What do you want?" Lawrence asked as soon as the sound of the front door shutting behind his sister ricocheted through the air.

Claude was silent for a split second longer than I was comfortable with, so I answered the question. "We're here to talk to you about your disappearance, Mr. Coates."

Sweat broke out on the man's forehead, and his voice was raspy when he responded. "Why? That was a long time ago. And I've already spoken to other police—"

"Whom you told nothing," Claude cut in.

Coates sneered. "Well, that's all I have to say about it."

I narrowed my eyes. He was hiding something, something big. And it was as apparent in his bravado as his obvious discomfort with our presence.

"Were you assaulted with a branding iron while you were missing, Mr. Coates?"

I gaped at Claude, as did Coates, who spluttered out something indecipherable. Way to jump to the punch line. Not only had he shown our hand, but he'd backed Coates into a corner. And most people didn't respond to that feeling by giving out information—not without wearing them down first, anyway.

"Get out of my house," Coates managed finally and turned away, and I cringed at his loud, screeching tone.

Claude moved faster than I'd ever seen him—ever seen anyone. And, in fact, moved so quickly I missed it. One second he was a few feet from Coates, with a couch and coffee table between them, and the next he was on the selkie.

I stared, my mind several seconds behind Claude. Claude grabbed at the selkie and Coates yelled an obscenity. The next thing I knew, Coates's shirt was on the floor, made of more pieces than it had been while on the selkie, and Claude had the man's arms behind his back, pretzel-like.

"Claude stop—let him go!" I took a step toward the men, but halted in my tracks. My hand automatically strayed to where I kept my sidearm, even though I was no longer carrying. But even if I had been, I wasn't entirely certain I had it in me to shoot Claude.

What could I do? Grab him? I wouldn't even register as a blip on the radar of an out-of-control vampire.

Claude growled and pushed the selkie away. Coates fell

to his knees, and I cringed in sympathy. He struggled up and turned to face us, wobbly on his hurt legs.

My feet moved again, almost of their own volition, and I reached to help the man up. But I stopped—as I had before—only this time for a very different reason.

Burned into the center of Coates's chest was a symbol I recognized.

The brand.

I looked at Coates's eyes—and the fear behind them bled through, almost palpable. He was muttering something softly, words I couldn't quite catch. With each syllable, his voice grew louder.

"...I don't remember!" Coates struggled back and fell against the arm of the couch. He sat on it, his face in his hands.

Dammit. His breath came quickly. Hyperventilating.

"Calm down, Mr. Coates. No one is going to hurt you." I shot Claude a warning glance, one that he pointedly ignored. Triumph lit his face.

Neither of us approached Coates at first. The selkie gathered his breath and tried to calm himself. I tried to do the same, but anger hit me at Claude's actions. We weren't criminals who would strip a man against his will, even of just his shirt. Even a liar like Coates.

I understood he wanted to make progress on the case—hell, I did, too. But there were lines, and he'd just crossed one of them. Screw crossed, he'd dove over and done cartwheels on the other side.

But I had to keep focused. Claude was a problem for later. With that in mind, I walked closer to Coates.

"Mr. Coates?" His breathing had slowed, but perspiration

covered his nearly bald head, and I could see skin connecting his fingers up to the first joint as he held his face. A sure sign of a selkie in distress. It was the first step before their joints joined and they transformed into seals. That he was still in human form given his emotional state was a testament to his control. A prince of some sort, indeed.

As I drew closer, he looked up from his hands. Obvious distress still colored his features, but he seemed calmer.

"I don't remember," he said, voice soft. "I don't remember that whole week. All I know is…" He took a deep breath. "When I think of talking about it, or if I even try thinking about it, a feeling of panic hits and I—"

"Can you walk us through it? Anything? The last thing you remember?"

"No—I told you. I don't remember." His voice grew fiercer, more panicked. "Just leave me alone!"

Claude moved between us—suddenly standing in front of the selkie—and I decided I really hated vampire speed.

"Tell us what you do know. We aren't leaving until you do."

The selkie started yelling again, his words turning indecipherable, and he faded into another panic attack. I grabbed Claude's shoulder and tugged him away from the selkie.

"He has to tell us something," he said before I could speak. Emotion that I'd never heard from the vampire rode his voice. Claude was rattled. "We need a next step."

"He can't. Look at him. Really look, Claude."

Doubt flickered across Claude's face, and he glanced at the selkie.

"There is nothing he's able to tell us, other than what he already has. But that could be a good thing."

"What?"

"Think about it. Something preventing him from speaking? Causing him to go into a panic attack when he tries to say too much? That stinks of magic. Maybe Natalie can make some sense of this. Use him to trace whoever created the spell."

He looked torn, his gaze all but dragged to the selkie.

"And, Claude." Bright blue eyes flickered back to me. "This isn't like you. This kind of pressure. You're hurting him." I kept my voice calm, even though I had to fight the urge to shake him, or slap some sense into him.

"Anymore."

"What?" I asked.

Something dark flickered across his features, but then it was gone, leaving only pained regret behind. "This isn't like me *anymore*."

Chapter Eight

If the drive to Wisconsin had been awkward, the drive back to Chicago was positively painful. Claude was obviously lost in thought, and far more distant and worried than I'd ever seen him. I swung back and forth between wanting to rage at him for treating the selkie like that, and telling him about my vision of Luc from when I was a child, just so he would let this go. How could I get him to give up his quest to prove the innocence of a man who was anything but?

And a third urge tugged at me. An urge that was far more dangerous than the others. I wanted to comfort him.

Because this case seemed to have shaken the confident vampire to his core. And something in me didn't like that one bit. But I couldn't comfort him, and I dared not show what I knew of Luc—that would risk him cutting me out of the case. Or worse, prompt a confrontation with the Magister before he was ready. Before he had backup in place. Before he had a plan.

Or worse, what if he stood by his friend regardless of what he'd done?

So I watched the darkening landscape fade from buildings, to naked trees and open spaces, and back to buildings even bigger than the ones we'd left behind, undecided and feeling like a wishy-washy loser.

We pulled into Claude's underground parking lot, and I shook my head to clear it. I'd dozed, nearly falling asleep.

"You still sleep during long drives," Claude murmured as he parked in the low-lit garage.

"You still talk about stuff that's none of your business." It wasn't much of a comeback, and he laughed. I frowned and exited the car. I'd need a little more time away from my almost-nap before I could think of a witty retort.

Claude didn't mention dinner, and neither did I. I could have rustled up something from his fridge, which appeared to be well-stocked. Or I could have demanded he order me something. Even after the day we'd had, he would have done so. But I wasn't interested in food.

I pulled a bottle of vodka out of his freezer and mixed it with Coke from the fridge. Claude walked in after taking a shower, his hair still damp, and watched me drink half the first cup in one long swallow.

"You crossed a line back there," I said.

"I know."

I waited a beat, but he didn't offer up anything else. No explanation. No promise that it would never happen again.

"That's it? That's all I get? You know? Well, fuck, Claude. Of course you know. You're not a damn idiot." I waved my glass at him. "At least I didn't think you were." Then I downed the other half.

Claude walked around the counter slowly. He took the glass from my hand and went about making me another drink.

"Have you ever been so obsessed with something that you couldn't see straight?" he asked. "That you couldn't see your future without it?"

"No," I lied. Why else was I here, working with Claude, if I wasn't a little bit obsessed myself. My brother's disappearance had ruined my childhood. My parents had gone from normal to fixated on keeping me safe. I'd grown to actually resent him—and that had made me hate myself a little bit.

And at times, when I was alone in the dark, I could almost admit I had a bit of an obsession for Claude that hadn't quite died.

But I'd never hurt anyone for my obsession, not an innocent.

"No?" He handed me the refilled glass and I grimaced. Okay, I kind of get it, But I would have never done what you did."

"Maybe you're just a better person than I am."

Fat chance of that. And then I said it. The question that was really bothering me. The one that had haunted my mind all the way back from Milwaukee. "What would you have done if I hadn't been there, Claude?"

He turned away from me and pressed his hands against the edge of the countertop. His head dropped, but I couldn't see his face. Couldn't decide what he might be feeling.

"I don't know." His voice was low and tired as if he carried a burden.

"I don't understand how branding a selkie gets Nicolas any closer to taking over as Magister."

"I haven't got all the answers yet, Beatrice. I'm still putting together the puzzle."

I hurt for him *although* we'd had such a short time together. Why did my body seem convinced that we'd forged a real connection? I set my drink down and walked to him. I slid a hand up his back, intending to offer him a small bit of comfort.

Claude had other ideas.

He turned, an emotion that looked somewhere between pain and determination on his face, and his mouth took mine. The kiss was laced with desperation and need, and passion flared at his touch. I wrapped my arms around his neck. He pulled me against him, then up. My legs went around his waist and he carried me the couple of steps to the countertop behind me.

The granite was hard and cold. My whole body ached, and his hands slid down my sides to cup my breasts through my shirt. I cried out against his mouth.

The gravity of what we were doing niggled at me, bringing doubt. It had taken me months to get him out of my system after our brief affair. Months to quit moping around when I wasn't working. Months to convince myself that it hadn't mattered. That he didn't matter.

It was all bullshit. But it was bullshit I had needed to believe.

At the same time, I couldn't bring myself to pull away as his lips slid down my neck, his fangs so close to my skin. I shuddered. And he growled against the tender skin of my collarbone.

"Need you," he said, his voice rough and full of an emotion I wasn't keen to examine.

I tilted his face to mine and took his mouth, trying to show him without words that I was just as desperate for him as he was for me. He drew me closer, one hand wrapped around my back and the other under my butt. His hardness pressed against me through our clothes, right where I needed him. I moaned, and then we were moving.

Pieces of clothing flew as we walked, with the vampire somehow coordinating the removal of my clothes without a single misstep. He set me down at the foot of his bed and I yanked his shirt over his head. His skin shone in the low light. Not as pale as vampires were reputed to be, but a touch different from a normal man. Muscles stretched beneath, corded and strong. Long and lean.

Just the way I liked him.

The rest of our clothes disappeared under feverish kisses. And then he was pushing me onto the bed, his mouth on my breast. I moaned as he pulled at my nipple, and his hand slipped between us to stroke me.

Sparks flashed almost immediately as the orgasm took me. I was almost embarrassed at how fast he could still do that to me, but his satisfied expression only made me need him again.

He brought my body back to the edge with his long fingers and clever tongue. I gripped his hardness and pulled him to me. I'd be damned if I came again without him.

Lips against my neck, he nuzzled me softly, body braced to enter mine.

"I need you, *mon chou*. All of you."

I knew what he was asking for—not just sex, but something perhaps even more intimate. I could have said no, and he would have respected it. But I'd never been able to tell him no. And desire for him to have me—in every way that he wanted—coiled inside me, tight and eager.

"Yes," I whispered.

He thrust his hips forward, filling me, forcing me to take all of him. A split second later, a sharp sensation stung my neck. Then he sucked.

Pain mixed with pleasure as he drove into me and pulled at my vein. Faster and harder. Thoughts evaded me, and I couldn't feel anything but him. Time stopped. The orgasm hit and rolled through me so powerfully I thought for a moment I couldn't handle it. Couldn't take it. Then Claude stiffened above me and buried himself inside my body. Taking his own pleasure, he cried out against my neck.

Minutes passed before I could think again. His weight still on me as he held me in the cradle of his arms. I sighed against his chest, and his hold tightened.

What the hell had I done?

The night passed like a dream. Like every bittersweet dream I'd had since Claude had ended things. But it wasn't a dream, and in the morning I woke to a belly full of regret, and the smell of something delicious.

Everyone knows that vampire bites are pleasurable. Everyone knows that bites can be addictive for the recipient and the vampire—even if it wasn't in the way that drugs are addictive, not to humans, at least.

Everyone knows that you never let a vampire bite.

Of course, this wasn't the first time I'd made that particular mistake with Claude.

I touched my neck in the mirror. Two small holes. They would disappear more quickly than most wounds, but it would be another day or two yet. They wouldn't scar. Thank goodness for scarf weather.

I knew better than to think they wouldn't scar me in other ways.

Claude waited for me in the kitchen, cooking waffles. Actual, made-with-a-waffle-maker waffles. The vampire seemed at ease, going through the motions of cooking with an extra skip in his step. Exactly the opposite of how I felt. Not that I didn't feel a bit de-stressed from our passionate night, but new stresses now replaced the old. He kissed my cheek when he handed me a plateful, and I offered him a small smile.

"The giant called while you were in the shower."

"Oh?" Focus on the case. For God's sake, focus on the case. But I couldn't seem to drag my gaze from his full lips. The memory of them on my body made me flush.

Amusement danced in Claude's eyes, but he kept to the topic at hand. "He has some information for us, thought we could head over this morning."

Some of my panic faded. Yes. This was good. We could pursue the case. I could pretend the night before never happened. It was a blip—I certainly wasn't falling for him again. I dug into my waffle. "Sounds good."

"Beatrice."

I looked up from my food and met his shining eyes, crinkled with pleasure. Hell, he had noticed my eyes on him. "That doesn't mean we're not talking about last night at some point."

Dammit. "There's nothing to talk about."

He grinned. The man's confidence knew no bounds. "Oh, there's plenty to talk about."

I attacked my waffle and ignored the weight of his stare, which I could feel following my every movement. We *didn't* have anything to talk about. Risking that feeling again—the emptiness and melodramatic sadness I'd felt before—wasn't going to happen. I was older now. Wiser.

And I'd been down that road.

So I ignored him through breakfast, and then we headed out. The drive to the metalworker's was quick, but my mood darkened as we drove, even as Claude's seemed to brighten. By the time we parked and Claude pushed quarters into the meter, I half expected the jerk to be humming.

But he didn't hum, although a smile lingered on his lips. As Chicago's bitter wind swept through my layers, I pulled my coat tighter around myself.

The metalworker answered the door quickly, as if he'd waited for us by the door, a sour expression on his face. His gaze met Claude's, and his frown deepened. The vampire hesitated at the door, then shot me a questioning glance before following the large man inside.

Again we trailed behind the man down a long, dark hallway into what had to be some sort of basement area. And again he sat. But this time, the walk didn't seem quite as fearsome, and the smell of smoke didn't bring to mind the brand and burning flesh.

"You said you had info for us," Claude said, settling into a chair not far from the counter. I remained behind him, suddenly feeling out of place.

The giant sighed heavily. "It's what I said."

Claude tensed, his body suddenly tight and unmoving.

"And?" All friendliness had disappeared from his tone. And what remained wasn't threatening, but all business.

"Yer not gonna want to hear this."

"Tell me."

"Found the metalworker that made the brand. Found its use."

"What was it used for?" I took a step toward them, tired of being left in the background. This was my case, too, whether Claude liked it or not. Whether he realized how important it was to me or not. Because it was important. More important than his beef with Nicolas.

"Torture. Looks like they was experimentin' with causing pain through the brand."

There were plenty of ways to torture people, both magical and mundane. Why leave a traceable mark behind? "Meaning what exactly?" I asked.

"Meaning they could do it from wherever. Whenever they cared to," Claude said.

"The fanger has the right of it."

"It forms a magical connection, then? They can cause a marked person pain from a distance?" Disbelief made my voice too loud, but I didn't care.

Claude turned to me. "That would be pretty damn useful. You'd be able to use it as a targeting system. Would be able to cause pain to the person marked whenever you liked, so long as they didn't alter the mark."

"Whoa, whoa." I shook my head vigorously. "No way. That kind of power over someone through a simple brand?"

"Nay. Yer misunderstanding. It's not so easy." The giant set the picture of the brand on the counter he used for a desk. "The brand is forged usin' witchcraft—powerful stuff, that. Can't be sensed. Can't be magically felt."

"But his sensitive partner felt the brand—" I began.

"Sure, bettin' she sensed the shaman power, though. The forgin' is only the first bit. Then they'd need some time with the poor soul caught in their web. Several days, I'd guess. And a shaman with as dark a soul as you can imagine to bind the spirit to the brand mark."

My stomach dropped. Several days. Shamanic power. But why? Who would want the ability to torture a selkie— even a selkie prince, or whatever he was—from afar? Surely there was little to be gained by it. And if torture had been their goal, then he probably wasn't the only one. Otherwise, why create a reusable brand?

"And bindin' the mark…" He shook his head. "It'd make it impossible to destroy on the poor man it was branded into."

"What about his memory issues?" Claude said. At the giant's questioning glance, he added, "The man can't remember what happened during the time he got the brand. Also has a tough time talking about it."

"Not shaman power, that. More witchcraft. Whoever be doin' this, he's goin' to a good deal of trouble."

"This all sounds like a fairy tale." I hadn't realized I'd spoken aloud until Claude replied.

"Not a fairy tale, but definitely something infinitely difficult to do. You'd need a shaman with no scruples, difficult to find in a spirit-based group of magic users. You'd need a witch powerful enough to pull it off—not easy to find among non-Covenant witches. Again without empathy, and an ability to work metal. And a witch—likely a different one—to work the forgetting spells, and the persuasion so he can't talk to anyone about it."

"Aye. And neither of them be a typical skill among witches."

"But you said you'd found the witch who made the brand," I pointed out. Hell, if we had that witch, we could no doubt track it further, to the person who'd orchestrated the whole thing. Although I was pretty sure I already knew who that was. Nicolas, maybe. But I didn't doubt his father was involved.

"Give me the name," Claude said, order clear in his tone.

"Nay. I won't be doin' that to 'em. And there's naught you can say to convince me otherwise."

Claude's face twisted, and within half a second he stood in front of the counter, directly across from the giant. He leaned toward him, hands gripping the counter, but the threat was clear.

The small bit of friendliness on the giant's face disappeared, and something wicked flashed behind his eyes.

"Dun try me, vampire. Friend or no, I ain't givin' you that name." He leaned back and crossed his arms, but I could see the sweat lacing his brow that hadn't been there before Claude moved. He was bluffing.

"But I got somethin' better for ya."

Claude's stare didn't soften one bit, and his focus looked unmovable.

"What's that?" I asked, but I didn't look away from Claude. What would happen if he attacked? I couldn't help either of them. Claude was one of the most powerful vampires in the country. But I would bet that one didn't get to be a metalworking witch without a heck of a lot of power.

Hell. If they fought I'd be lucky to get out of the damn

building before it collapsed around them.

My chest twinged at the idea. Would Claude fight the witch, oblivious to how easily damaged my human body was? Was he more interested in getting to Nicolas than my safety?

I didn't think I wanted to know the answer to that question.

The witch's gravelly voice broke the tension with a simple phrase. "I know who it was that commissioned the brand, so you'll not need to seek out the witch."

I sucked in a breath of smoke-tinged air. "Who?"

Claude pulled back, blinking as if stunned there wasn't going to be a fight.

The witch, as if keen on dramatics, pulled a cigar from the top drawer of his makeshift desk and trimmed the end. "Was none other than the man his self." He lit the cigar and sucked in a quick breath of smoke, then blew it out between yellowing rows of teeth. "The man who bought it was the Magister, Luc Chevalier."

Chapter Nine

Claude flew at the man. There was simply no other word for it, even if the logical part of my brain knew that vampires couldn't actually fly. My breath stuck in my throat, and for a split second I felt like I was caught in one of my visions. Caught watching images that had already occurred. Caught without the ability to change anything. All I could do was stand witness as Claude killed the witch.

But then I was moving.

Claude gripped the man by his collar, and was yelling. Calling the witch a liar.

I grabbed Claude's arm and yanked with all my strength. He didn't move an inch.

"Claude, let him go." I tried to keep my voice calm. Panicking wouldn't do anything but add fuel to the explosive situation. But when he didn't even turn to look at me, some of the fear I felt crept into my voice. "Claude!"

The vampire turned his head and blinked at me. He

dropped the giant, and I realized that he'd actually been supporting the man's weight. The giant fell back against one of his elevated fire pits, leaning against it for support.

"Use your words," I told him. The vampire didn't crack a smile, but something came back into his eyes. Something I recognized.

"Get out," the giant managed to choke out. "I won't pursue ya, we've been friends so long. But I dun want to see you in here again for some years."

I tugged Claude toward the door. He turned back when we hit the threshold. And when he spoke, his voice sounded hollow.

"You're sure about this?"

"Aye."

"Sorry about your neck," Claude muttered, and then allowed me to lead him away.

I took his keys and drove us to a small restaurant I'd enjoyed the last time I was in Chicago. They served deep-dish pizza. I wasn't hungry. But I wasn't ready to be alone with Claude, either. Not until he no longer looked so dazed.

We sat in a corner. It was still early, only ten forty-five, so the place was practically empty. I ordered the first pizza I saw on the menu in an effort to get the waiter to leave us alone.

"He was lying." Claude's hollow voice hurt my heart. I reached across the table, took his hand in mine, and gave it a squeeze.

"Could be." I didn't think so, but Claude just looked so miserable. And as an investigator, it was my job to look at all the angles. "Let's say for argument's sake that Luc isn't responsible. Let's say it's Nic. How would torturing that man get him any closer to taking over as Magister? Unless…" I almost didn't want to voice the thought. I hated adding to his hope when it was pretty obvious that the Magister was as dirty as his son and Claude needed to accept it.

"Unless?"

"Well, you said something about local otherworlder leader support, right?" I shrugged. "I don't know. Maybe some kind of mental conditioning is at work here. I mean, the man was spelled not to talk about the week he was gone. Could he somehow be conditioned into supporting Nic in a coup?"

A tiny bit of hope lit up his eyes and my heart jumped.

"I've never heard of such a thing, but I'm redefining what's possible with this case. Last week I would have said that torturing someone from a distance with a brand and shamanic magic was impossible."

"Don't get your hopes up too high. I still think Luc's in the thick of this." It hurt to say, but it had to be said.

"Luc is the only constant. The only person who has been in my life since the change. The only one who has cared about me at all."

"That's not true."

He glanced up at my hard tone, and gave me a good facsimile of his normal grin. "Maybe not. But he has been like a brother to me. I can't imagine him being involved in this. And, it's a scary thought."

"What is?"

"That I might truly be alone in the world."

The waiter dropped off the Cokes I'd ordered with the pizza and I nodded to him in thanks. Truth was, I wanted to hug the man for interrupting before I could say something stupid to Claude. Something to take some of the pain from his voice. Something I wasn't sure I was ready to say.

"Look, Claude. I get that he's like a brother to you. But you're going to have to put your big boy pants on and deal with this."

He snorted. A small sound, but I'd take it.

"Maybe you're right. Maybe I'm an idiot for ignoring the evidence." He shook his head. "One way or another, I'll find out for sure."

Now that, I didn't like the sound of. "Look—"

"Thank you. For staying with me through this. I haven't… I haven't been as good a man as I should have been with you." The fervor in his voice and expression stunned me into silence. What the hell was I supposed to say to that?

"Damn straight," I said finally.

His confident grin slipped back onto his face and I almost sagged against the table in relief. Dealing with Claude so out of his normal character was exhausting. I worried about him far more than I should.

"So. I think I should spend some more time with the brand this afternoon. Maybe you can focus on shamans who might have been able to attach it to a person's spirit, and who might have that kind of inclination. Hell, that kind of power on top of being an evil son-of-a-gun can't be a common combination among shamans," I said.

"I'd imagine not."

"Good." And maybe tonight I'd talk to him about my first vision of Luc. I couldn't talk to him about it here. Too public. Too exposed. I was too chicken.

I needed time to gather my courage.

And with the smell of pizza filling the air, I was getting

hungry. I needed to eat before I talked about it. Needed to formulate responses to his questions—questions I knew he'd ask. Like I didn't tell him when I first saw Luc in the vision from the brand—because I didn't trust him to let me stay on the investigation. Because I wasn't entirely sure I trusted him?

Yeah. I needed time to come up with some better answers. At least, more tactful ones. More certain ones.

I wished I had some handy.

"Maybe we can open a bottle of wine when we're done. Talk through what we know," I mused aloud. Maybe we could do more than open a bottle of wine. No. What was I thinking? Last night was a mistake. Not one I was willing to repeat. Not one I could repeat if I wanted to keep myself at a distance. Safe from the feelings he elicited in me without even trying.

"That sounds delightful," he said gruffly, "but I'm afraid that I'll have to leave you on your own tonight. Although I'd be happy to—"

"What? Why?"

"The gala is tonight."

I just stared. "Seriously? You're going to Luc's house for a party. With all this going on?"

"Yes." He sipped his Coke and made a yuck face.

"What's wrong with your drink?"

"Nothing. Just not the best thing I've tasted today." He winked at me.

"Fuck, Claude. You're not distracting me with that B.S." Heat crawled up my neck. Damn vampire, anyway. "Going to this party is a stupid, risky idea."

"Why? No one knows we're investigating the brand.

No one knows I'm looking into Nic—not any more than I usually am. And"—he cleared his throat—"no one knows we're looking at Luc."

He had a point, but I didn't have to like it. At least he was more on board with looking into the Magister.

"This will be a perfect opportunity to do a little recon. To chat with them in a comfortable setting," he said.

"Good point. I'll go with you."

"No. I'm not risking you, frail human." A wicked smile flashed at the silly insult.

I grinned back, unable to help myself. "You just said it yourself. It's not risky. It's not a stupid idea. So you have no reason not to take me."

He gaped for a second before his mouth snapped shut. "You haven't been invited."

"I'm sure they'll allow you a plus one."

"I don't—"

"Bring me or I'll find my own way in. Like you said, it's a perfect opportunity for some recon. And I'm going. Do you really want me to get caught trying to shimmy in through a window? How embarrassing would that be?"

The waiter interrupted Claude's response, dropping a piping hot pizza onto the middle of our table. The smell made my mouth water.

"I'm not winning this argument, am I?"

I reached for the spatula, slipped it under a slice of pizza, and scooped it onto my plate. "Nope."

Convincing Claude, as it turned out, was the easy part.

The harder part proved to be finding a dress in time that I didn't totally hate and could actually afford. After refusing Claude's offer to shop with me, I finally found one at a Nordstrom at the Shops at North Bridge. It was sleeveless. Even better, it had an Asian-style neckline that was just high enough to cover part of what was left of the bite mark he'd left low on my neck. I'd have to cover the fading marks with makeup to be sure.

The cocktail dress was quite pretty, black and short and it fit my slender body just so. I had no doubt that it would look low-class and simple compared to many of the Magister's guests. But I shouldn't be terribly underdressed, not enough to be noticed, if Claude was right about the gala's tone. Besides, I didn't have thousands of dollars to waste on a dress I would only wear for one night. A night of spying on vampires, no less.

It would just have to do.

I packed it up with a pair of shoes and a clutch that I'd found in the same store, then took a cab back to Claude's. The doorman barely glanced at me and my dress bag, and I was back up to the condo without a hitch.

Claude wasn't in any of the common areas. A couple of hours yet until I had to get ready, so I decided to spend some quality time with the brand. Pleasant or no, it might be useful. Besides, I needed to think of anything but the vampire. The horrible torture of a selkie would do the trick.

The second I touched the brand the world around me disappeared. White noise rushed through my ears and blackness filled my sight. Then the brand burst into my field of vision, bright and almost painful to look at. Panic and confusion hit me like a punch to the gut.

Then the Magister.

His face filled my vision, anger twisted his mouth, and I tried to cringe away. The vision rolled back, flashing and moving like a stop-motion film half shot. The brand was in his hand — still attached to the long handle that had once held it. He yanked at it, yelling words I couldn't hear. Clouded by the darkness of the vision's edge, another person gripped the brand, too. Were they fighting over it? I couldn't make any sense of it, too much fear. Too much panic. Needed to run.

The clatter of the brand hitting Claude's coffee table startled me, and I gasped for air. Then an arm slipped behind me and Claude sat next to me on the couch. He pulled me close to him, his strong body supporting mine. His scent surrounded me and filled my lungs.

I leaned into him, unable to resist the comfort when the vision was so fresh. Panic still tumbled through me, making me want to turn and run. But it wasn't something that I could run from. I'd carry the vision within myself.

Always.

Chapter Ten

The vision had shaken me more than I wanted to admit. So when it came time to get ready for the party, my hands trembled when I tried to do my makeup. No matter how I tried, my eyeliner refused to go on right, and no way could I use my mascara. It took a heck of a lot of smoothing to make me presentable, but I got the added bonus of a smoky look around my eyes, courtesy of the need to smudge everything together so that my squiggly lines couldn't be seen by the world.

Claude watched me walk the hallway from my room like a high school boy watching his prom date descending the stairs, wide-eyed and with hopeful passion in his eyes. Nerves fluttered in my stomach at the sight of him, too. And for half a second I forgot. I forgot that we were only friends—if that. I forgot that we were headed to a dangerous gala where a sociopath waited. I forgot that we weren't in love.

And in that moment, the expression on Claude's face made me think he forgot, too.

His gaze slid slowly down my body, as if he had all night to take me in. Then his eyes met mine, and I could see so many things reflected in those light blue depths. Desire that made my stomach tighten. But something else, too. He looked almost hopeful.

"You're beautiful, *mon chou*," he murmured when I got close.

He didn't look so shabby himself. Hair styled back from his face revealed his strong jaw and bright eyes in a way that he normally hid. The suit tailored to his long, lean body revealed the breadth of his shoulders, and hinted at the strong muscles of his chest and legs. He was a panty-dropping hunk of vampire. He told me that I looked beautiful but he looked like he'd come from another world.

"Let's go," I said, then swallowed to clear the lump from my throat. I had to stymie this line of thought. Sure, the man was pretty. But I'd be damned if I had to dwell on it.

I reached for the clutch I'd bought with the dress and shoes, and paused when I saw my hand visibly shake. I shouldn't have.

Claude intercepted my hand, taking it with his own. His cool thumb slid across my skin.

"You're shaking."

"I'm fine."

"Does this happen often with visions?"

Too often. "I'm just rundown. Can we go, please?" There was a desperate note in my voice that I didn't like one bit. If I caved with Claude, I'd have to admit how I felt about him. And I wasn't entirely sure that I trusted him any longer. He was a good man—he was. Even if he had been a misguided jerk to me once. But he'd also proven that he trusted the wrong people. And that misplaced trust could screw us both.

That dangerous hand gripped mine for a moment longer, then he pulled it to his lips and brushed them against my skin. My breath caught, and a shiver ran through my body that had nothing to do with the vision.

"We could be fashionably late," he said, voice low and smooth.

The idea sounded good—too good. Being with Claude would bring me back from the vision, give me something to concentrate on that was very real, and very overwhelming. I wanted to stay and make love to him so badly that it twisted my gut and made my fingertips tingle.

And that's exactly why I couldn't.

"No," I finally managed. "We have work to do."

Despite Claude's offhand assertion that we weren't already fashionably late, the party was in full swing when we arrived. A harried valet took Claude's keys, and classical music flowed from the large manor the Magister called home.

"Seems like an odd time of year for a big party like this."

"He has several throughout the year. A good opportunity to politic, and to remind people who is in charge."

"Not sure I'd invite people I planned on threatening into my home."

Claude grinned. "The main house is actually on the other side of the property. This is sort of a ballroom area with guest suites. It's used a lot for official visitors—other Magisters, their people. Visiting dignitaries and such."

Of course the Magister had more than one house on the

same property. Who didn't?

A blast of cold air hit me. Why hadn't I thought to buy a wrap? My jacket had been too casual to wear with the dress, and I'd shrugged off Claude's offer to stop somewhere on the way. But thankfully the distance from the valet station to the front door was short, and I'd worn my coat from Claude's condo until his car had warmed up.

Luck proved to be on my side though, because warmth flooded me as soon as I cleared the door into the manor. Whether due to the vampires' rather useful tolerance for temperature variations that exceeded that of us normals, or because they were trying just a little too hard to combat the frigid Chicago cold, they had the thermostat set just perfect for a human in a cocktail dress sans wrap. Convenient, and probably meant that this party catered to a mixed otherworlder crowd, like the giant said.

"You ready?" Claude asked, offering me his arm.

I took it and a tingle ran through me at the touch. Just the cold bothering me. It wasn't anticipation; it was the beginning of frostbite.

"Wow," I muttered when we hit the main ballroom after traveling down a short hallway and passing a coat check along the way.

The vampires and their guests were impressive. Dresses of every shape and current fashion graced the hall. Nothing vintage, like I'd thought we might see. Vampires, it seemed, did not dwell on the past.

At least not in a public forum.

Music flowed, not from a jukebox or DJ, but from a small group of men in tuxedos with string instruments held close to their bodies and sweat touching their shining foreheads.

And waiters, also in tuxes, distributed drinks in crystal glasses, and several types of appetizers. I was happy to see that while some women wore evening gowns that sparkled against the low lighting, others wore cocktail dresses not too dissimilar from my own.

"It's like something from a movie." I kept my voice low, but vampires had excellent hearing.

"Thank you, my dear. I'm glad that someone appreciates all of the trouble my kind assistant has gone to." The voice was unfamiliar, confident, and deep. "Please, Claude, introduce us."

Claude shifted a step back, so I could see the man who approached from his left.

The air left my lungs, and my stomach dropped.

I knew every tiny line around those eyes. The way the light glinted off his thick hair. I had seen that falsely young, handsome face in my nightmares since I was ten years old. Nightmares that had returned with renewed force since I'd touched that brand.

"Of course. *Maître*, this is my date and friend, Beatrice Davis. Beatrice, this is Luc Chevalier, our host for the evening and the area Magister."

I managed to mutter something appropriate, and I hoped that the Magister considered my tongue-tied nature a compliment. That his station and power had overwhelmed me. After all, the Magister didn't know me to be anything other than Claude's date. For all he knew, I was easily impressed by vampires—especially Magisters.

"I need to speak with you alone for a moment, Claude. If you don't mind, my dear."

The Magister wasn't really seeking my permission, but

he was polite, I'd give him that. I nodded, trying to keep a smile on my face, since I couldn't bring myself to speak.

"Would you like me to bring you back a drink?" Claude asked.

"Sure," I managed.

"Wonderful. I'll show you around afterward." Claude gave me a tight smile.

Just seeing the Magister's face, so familiar and yet brand-new, sent emotions rushing through me. Anger and rage carried by a flurry of questions I wanted—needed—answered. Questions about the selkie and the brand and what the hell he'd been doing in the room when the brand was imprinted with that vision.

Questions about my brother.

But I couldn't ask any of them. So I pushed down the anger and swallowed the lump in my throat.

"No rush, I can mingle just fine." I gave him a broad smile that I hoped looked bright, and not full of barely concealed rage.

Claude and the Magister disappeared into the crowd, and I grabbed a glass of champagne from the waiter. I swallowed a bit, just to fit in with the other guests, and barely withheld a grimace. There was no doubt the champagne was good, definitely expensive. But I hated the taste. Just not my drink.

The crowd was full of interesting-looking people, vampire women with their perfect skin and rich furs, and the occasional vampire man, skin just slightly too pale. Although there were surprisingly few actual vampires. What were the others? Humans? Witches? Perhaps a mix of just about every type of otherworlder.

I almost wished for the powers of a sensitive so I could tell for sure. There were hints. A twitchy woman in the corner who moved like an imp. Two women—sisters by the look of them—that radiated so much sex appeal I was tempted to ask them to dance. Succubi, then.

Did the Magister keep the vampire numbers down purposefully in these mixed-group balls in order to keep the auras of fear manageable? I guessed it wasn't good manners to force your guests to concentrate on not running from the room the whole night.

They all looked rich, happy, and delighted to have been invited. But how many attended just to socialize, and how many for other purposes? Backstabbing and deal-making were doubtlessly the main reason most were here, I'd bet my badge on it.

I sidestepped a portly man wearing so much cologne that I almost gagged, and then stopped in my tracks. A handsome man stood about twenty feet from me, a break in the crowd allowing me to see him clearly. Like most of the men, he wore a tuxedo and was undoubtedly good-looking. But it was his resemblance to Luc Chevalier that caught my eye.

A younger version of the Magister—although in appearance he only looked ten years shy of Luc—the man had probably been changed in his early twenties. The same nose and hair, the same jawline and general height. But unlike the Magister, this man had a cruel turn to his lips, as if he could either laugh or order a murder with his next breath.

There was no doubt in my mind that I was looking at the Magister's son—at Nicolas Chevalier. I could see why Claude suspected him of murder, and who knew what else. He might look human, but he wore cruelty like a cloak.

Or maybe I was only seeing what I expected to see?

I scanned the room for Claude, but the vampire had effectively disappeared. Nicolas turned and started for the far end of the ballroom, away from the entrance. Giving the ballroom one last glance for Claude, I followed.

A subtle pursuit, it was not. I did my best to move through the crowd as if at random, but the vampire was moving quickly toward a hallway and I had to struggle to keep up. I slipped inside after him. A woman in a red dress with a slit up to her waist strutted past me, headed back for the ballroom. The way my eyes wanted to follow her made her succubus nature obvious. A man passed me as well, not even sparing me a glance. Definitely a vampire—my heart rate kicked up a notch at the intimidation flowing from his aura.

Nicolas moved even faster, and I trotted after him, passing a powder room and a small balcony where smokers gathered. The noise from the ballroom faded behind me, and when I took a turn I'd sworn the vampire had taken, the noise completely disappeared. Had to be a noise-dampening spell.

The thought slowed my pace. Those spells worked both ways. Were they trying to keep the noise out, or in? Since I hadn't seen another partygoer for a couple of turns, I was hoping for out. But its presence made me nervous.

Sure, they weren't uncommon in a nice household like this. They could be used to keep the noise from the party away from the guest quarters. But what if this spell's purpose was darker?

I moved as silently as I could down the long hallway, which was lit by low-watt bulbs set in small sconces along the wall. For a second, I thought I'd gone the wrong way. But another step and I could feel sweat break out on my forehead, and I had the sudden urge to run.

The intimidating aura of a vampire.

Was it Nicolas? If so, the man really had a nasty aura.

Not a peep sounded until I hit another corner. The voices coming out of the room at the end of the short hall were low and hurried, and I couldn't make out the words. A small bit of light shone through the corner of the slightly open doorway where the muffled voices came from.

I crept forward, thankful for the rug that lined the floor. How close could I get without the vampire inside noticing I was here? The smart thing to do would be to leave. Because if they caught me, I would be worse than dead.

That thought sank in. *What the hell was I doing?* Sure, I was an investigator, but I was more the "touch things and research online" type—less the "chase bad guys without even a sidearm to my name" type. I turned to go, but a single word, ringing clearly from behind the door, stopped me.

Claude.

I couldn't convince my body to leave after that. What if the people behind that door were plotting to off Claude, and I missed the details because I was too afraid to listen in? Even if they caught me, surely they wouldn't kill me with a houseful of guests only a few turns down the hall?

The sound-dampening spell was something I decided to ignore, however. Wouldn't do to dwell on the fact that no one outside of this area could hear me scream.

Creeping forward slowly, I kept my breathing as quiet as possible. Tempting as it was to hold my breath, that wouldn't do. I'd end up gasping for air and giving myself away as surely as if I walked in that door and demanded to know what was going on.

The voices grew clearer as I approached.

"…doesn't have anything."

"He has the brand, made by my own hand. That ain't enough for ya? The timetable ain't bendable now, fanger. We don't have time for bullshit."

My hands clenched into fists automatically, and I had to force myself to stay put. I recognized that voice. The urge to fling open the door and ask them what the hell they were up to threatened to overrun my good sense, but I couldn't let it. I had no gun. No useful otherworlder powers. And no one would hear my screams.

"That isn't proof, and my father will not act without direct and incontrovertible proof." The smooth drawl that could only be the Magister's son's was so full of confidence I wanted to slap it right out of him.

"I'm not worried about yer father! It's that fuckin' vampire cop. He's got a hankerin' for ya, and a psychometrist followin' him around like a lapdog."

A surge of anger hit, but I kept my mouth shut. The voices lowered, indecipherable. My welcome was more than worn out. I needed to get away and tell Claude what I'd heard before they noticed me. I stepped back, but my heel caught on the carpet. My hand slammed against the wall as my body did its best not to fall.

Hell.

I turned and rushed down the hall as quietly as I could. It was possible they'd inspect the hall if they'd heard me, then look no further.

Not likely.

But it was the only hope I had, so I clung to it as I ran down the winding halls.

Chapter Eleven

Two turns later, I was still running down the hall. Panic over-rode my desire to play it cool. When I took what had to be my fourth wrong turn, I ran headlong into a hard chest. I would have flopped ungracefully to the ground, but the man grabbed my arms and held me to him. I struggled against the impossible strength. How had they gotten ahead of me? With all the wrong turns I'd no doubt made, it was no wonder they'd headed me off.

"Let. Me. Go!" I yanked with all my strength and the man did just that, sending me flying, only to bend down just in time to catch me in his arms. Striking green eyes, laced in amusement, met mine.

"Are you all right?" the Magister asked.

I couldn't seem to find any words.

He pulled me to my feet, and I fought against the urge to push him away. Was he here to help me? Hurt me? Was it possible that of all the people present at this big party, I'd only accidentally run into Luc Chevalier?

Unlikely.

"My apologies," I managed. "Got lost on the way to the ladies' room. I'll just be getting back to the party."

"I'll guide you. I'd hate for you to get lost again."

"Oh, gosh, no thank you." What to say? My mind raced and I struggled not to yell at him, ask him what had happened to my brother. A lot of good that would do me, in an empty hallway of a house I'd gotten lost in, with his likely murderous son and evil witch at my heels. "I wouldn't want to inconvenience you."

"It's no inconvenience." His mouth tightened. "I insist."

I took a step back—or tried to. The Magister grabbed my elbow, his hand tight on my skin. I opened my mouth to yell when someone touched my back, making me jump.

"Everything all right here, Luc?" Claude's smooth voice had never sounded so damn good.

Luc's smile returned, but tension remained around his eyes. "Of course. I was just about to help your friend find her way back to the party."

"I'll assist her."

Luc hesitated, then nodded. "Of course." Then to me he added, "Enjoy your evening, my dear. Please do take care not to get lost again."

His words still hanging in the air, Luc gave us a short bow and then turned and left. But he didn't head back the way he'd come—instead he went in the direction I'd come from.

I waited until Luc was out of sight, then whispered, "We have to go."

"What were you doing back here?" he asked, his voice

low, too. "Skulking and plotting, no doubt."

"Claude," I said, barely able to stop myself from stomping at him. I could hardly voice my worries aloud, when Nicolas could be lurking around the next corner, so I glared at him with my heart still racing and fear making me ready to jump out of my skin.

My look seemed to do the trick. The amusement faded from his expression and a very un-Claude-like seriousness took its place. Without another word, he took my elbow with his right hand and led me down the hallway; his eyes darted quickly across the space as we walked, alert for danger.

Obviously familiar with the layout of the house, Claude led me through the maze of hallways until we hit a door. Freezing wind hit me and I blinked against it. A near full moon lit a courtyard area around us, revealing trees, benches, and plants, all washed of color by the snow and moonlight. Claude's coat came around my shoulders. Before I could thank him, we were moving again.

Relief had hit me when I saw Claude, but that relief faded as we walked. I knew he could protect me better than just about anyone else, but he was cautious and silent.

We weren't home free yet.

The stone path was well kept and had only a brush of snow on it. Claude held my elbow again, and I had no doubt that if I slipped he'd catch me before I could touch the ground. So I moved with confidence, keeping up with the vampire's quick pace.

We reached a gate and Claude flipped a latch. The gate opened, revealing a very well lit parking lot. Lamps like you'd see in a commercial lot lined the area, though they were a bit short and more stylishly done than most I'd seen.

Claude's car started before we reached it, and he helped me into the passenger's side before taking his place in the driver's seat. I almost bit his head off for it. I didn't appreciate chivalry when it came to things I was more than capable of doing for myself, but I held my tongue.

Now was not the time to bitch.

"What happened?" he asked once we were on the road.

"Why did you already have your keys?"

"I carry a spare set. I'll have to go back for the other set later."

I glanced out at the naked trees flying by. Long shadows lurked, ready to jump out at us at any second, flashing fang and steel.

"Beatrice?"

"I saw Nicolas Chevalier at the party."

"And?"

"And I…I followed him when he went down a hallway."

"You what?"

"He looked like he was up to no good." Not a great defense, but true.

I risked a glance at the vampire. Unhappy didn't begin to cover the tension in his frame and the thin line formed by his mouth.

"What? I'm an investigator. I was following a lead."

"You're an investigator who isn't on a case. You're an investigator who is currently on leave. You're an investigator without even a sidearm following a known killer—who also happens to be a vampire—down a secluded hallway."

"I didn't say it was secluded," I huffed and crossed my arms. What did he know anyway? Just because I wasn't technically on a case didn't mean the investigative part of my brain turned off. Besides, this was the most important case I'd ever worked on, whether he knew it or not.

"Was it?"

"Look, do you want to talk about how stupid you think it was, or do you want to listen to what I found out?"

He grinned and my body clenched in response. "Lady's choice."

Whatever. I was not going to fall before his charm. "I overheard Nicolas talking to your giant friend."

"That's impossible. He hates the Chevaliers, especially Nic."

"He lied. Or he doesn't like you more. Or, hell, maybe he just likes money more than he hates the lot of you." I shivered and pulled Claude's coat tighter. "They were talking about you. And they called me a fucking lapdog." I tried to keep the outrage from my voice, but failed.

Claude laughed loudly, body shaking. I burned with anger, tugging on my hair and too pissed off to speak. I wasn't entirely sure if I was mad at Claude or just the man who'd called me a lapdog, but Claude was closer and the way I was feeling I was more than willing to use him as a punching bag.

He laughed long enough I almost told him to pull over, lest he run us off the road, but finally his amusement faded enough that he could talk again.

"What else did they say?"

I just glared at him.

"You're not a lapdog, sweet. That's why it's so damn hilarious." He shot me a sexy smile and his voice lowered. "If anything, you're a tiger."

The scenery outside suddenly became very interesting to me.

"So, did you get anything else?"

"Sounded like your friend was the one who made that brand. And Nic said something about not being worried about you, that his father wouldn't act without proof. Like, doubt-free proof."

"That much I know." He pulled into the parking garage of his building.

"The giant also mentioned that they were locked into a schedule. Things couldn't be moved now. Something like that."

His face was grave when he looked at me, and I hoped some of the paleness was due to the ugly fluorescent lighting of the parking garage. "My sources and evidence were right. Something big is going down soon."

"Seems like it."

"I need to call Natalie."

"The witch? Why?" I asked.

"She's Covenant. The giant falls under her purview."

"Seriously? You're going to let someone else bring this guy in?"

His smile turned dark. "The Covenant doesn't bring dark witches in, *mon chou*. And I'm not concerned with him. Nicolas is my problem. I'll let the witches deal with their own garbage."

The shower made me feel better, as if fear was washable and I could scrub it off to swirl down the drain. Not likely. But at least I could wash away the sweat. I felt safe in Claude's con-do though, which struck me as especially stupid and further proof that my body couldn't be trusted.

Not that I thought Claude couldn't handle himself. For all of his humor and playful attitude, the vampire was not a man to be trifled with. But if Nicolas came, he wouldn't come alone.

However, the Magister's son struck me as subtler than that. As a man who worked in the shadows. I didn't think he'd strike so openly even if he did suspect we knew something.

"Hey," I said when I emerged into the living room. Claude had the fireplace going. A gas fireplace, but pretty nonetheless. Calming. He handed me a glass of dark red wine, and watched me over the rim of his glass.

I didn't guzzle the wine, but I certainly sipped a bit faster than normal. Not that I'd get drunk—talk about a stupid idea when a vampire might want you dead for hearing too much—but a little bit would calm my nerves.

"Are you well?"

No, I wasn't well. There was little doubt that Nicolas had heard me when I ran from his room, and likely even before that when I tripped like a clumsy oaf. Damn heels, anyway.

"I'm fine. Just—" Freaked out. Scared shitless. Angry as hell. "—tired."

"Tired?" He gave me a lazy smile. "How tired?"

I took another drink of my wine. I wasn't ready to deal with the "us question," but I also wasn't sure that I could continue sleeping with him with the question still in the air. Not that there was even a question. I was done with him. Shit.

"Did you call Natalie?" I asked instead.

"Yes. She's been working with the selkie, Coates. She's made some headway there."

"I'm surprised that he's allowing it. She must be more charming than you were."

"He's freaked out enough to allow her to try to help. For now."

"We should go to the police. It's time to call in backup, Claude."

"We can talk about that in the morning," he said. But there was a finality in his tone. He was humoring me. This was his personal vendetta, not something he wanted police involvement in. No witnesses. No arrests.

Did I feel differently about my need to bring in Luc Chevalier and question him about my brother? I wasn't sure.

There were still so many things I didn't know. Like what exactly Natalie hoped to gain by examining the selkie—information, or freedom for him from the spell conditioning? Or, what was our next step, if not going to the police? But the look in Claude's eyes halted my questions. And brought my thoughts back to him. Back to us.

But mostly back to him.

He approached me slowly, as if giving me time to run away if that's what I wanted. And logically I knew that was the right thing to do. Because he was unattainable, and he got to me on a level that no man ever had. Because he'd hurt me before. Because he could so easily hurt me again.

But every instinct in my body urged me to stay.

My body was a damn traitor.

"Claude—"

"He could have hurt you, you know. Done things that you can't imagine. Things he's been tied to in the past. Death would have been a blessing."

"First, I'm an OWEA agent. I can imagine a lot.

Second—"

He touched my lips with his fingertip, silencing me. I wondered what he would do if I slipped the tip into my mouth and bit it. I knew he wanted me—he'd proven that. But did he want me with the same intensity—the same fire— that drove me back to him when I should have run away?

"Do you know what would have happened to me if I'd lost you?"

Hope surged within me, unbidden and most unwelcome. Maybe he did feel something for me. Something powerful and real. Something like what I dared not admit—even to myself—I felt for him.

"You are my responsibility, you know." His words smudged my hopes, but didn't dash them. Need coated his expression, under the worry.

Need that I felt vibrating through every inch of my body.

"Is that all I am? Your responsibility?" A silly question. A girl's question. And I was no girl. Not the one he'd had an affair with.

I kind of missed that girl. She'd been an optimist. A cheerleader. A believer in great love.

"Ah, *mon chou*." He slid the back of his fingers down my jawline and over my throat, his touch so soft I barely felt it. And his gaze weighed even more heavily on me, filled with such need that I barely believed my own eyes.

Did my eyes reveal the same?

"You never understood the way I felt. I made sure of that. You still don't. And maybe that's for the best." He closed his eyes, and when he opened them again, some of his normal amusement was there. My stomach sank. His guard was back up.

And I needed to put mine back up, too. To step away. To go to bed. Alone.

But when he lowered his face to mine, almost painfully slow, all I could do was tilt my chin to meet him.

His mouth touched mine softly, feather light before moving away, then another light touch. I ached for him, and tried to push harder against his lips, but he held me firm, intent on his soft assault.

Still moving slowly, he tugged off my clothes, one piece at a time, leaving soft kisses in his wake. He pulled off my bra, then knelt in front of me and continued his soft attack on my breasts.

"Claude," I muttered. I gripped his hair and turned his face up so I could meet his gaze. I didn't say anything else, but I knew he could read the need in my eyes.

"I love the way you say my name," he said, his voice rough with need. "When I'm inside you, your blood filling my mouth, I forget myself. My past. My need for anything but you."

Bet you say that to all the girls was on my tongue, but the glib joke didn't make it past my lips. His eyes shone in the dark when he looked at me, reflecting his feelings without guile.

"When you didn't return my call, I almost came for you. I wanted to drag you back. Force you to accept my apology. Convince you to love me."

The world stopped, and then spun. I gripped his shoulders and took a long breath. "Claude—"

"Whatever happens. You should know that."

Dread rose in my stomach, mixing with my desire, curdling it. *Whatever happens.* What exactly did he think was going to happen? I couldn't make myself ask the question though, couldn't ruin the moment.

"I would have gone with you. If you had come," I said finally.

A smile peeked out from his cloud of emotions, and he laughed softly. "Ah, mon amour, I'm glad to know that."

Even though it's too late.

He didn't say it, but I heard the words all the same.

And then his mouth was on mine, no longer gentle. He took what he needed from me, and I took from him. Desperate to have him all around me, I wrapped my arms around his neck and my legs around his waist. He carried me, I thought toward the bedroom, but we only made it as far as his dining room table.

I pulled his shirt off, then struggled with his belt, only managing to push his pants down just enough for his cock to spring free. He pushed his tongue against mine, mouth bruising my lips, and I gripped his hardness. Satisfaction swept through me when he moaned, long and low.

Then, hands on my hips, he pulled me to the edge of the table and thrust into me with one hard, swift motion. I cried out at the sudden fullness.

This time he didn't ask. His teeth pierced my breast near my nipple, and he sucked the wound and the nipple hard. The orgasm hit me immediately, spiraling through me as he pumped into me harder and faster with every beat of my heart. I held on to his neck with one hand, and pressed the other behind me for balance as pleasure hit me in waves.

His fingers digging into my hips, he shouted my name against my breast, then stilled.

Minutes passed, then he pulled me into a tight hug. Face

buried in my neck, he took a deep breath. A fuzzy haze of pleasure enveloped me, and his scent filled my lungs. And for a moment, hope pierced my worry. Maybe we could make it through this together. Maybe we could take down Nicolas and find out what happened to my brother. Maybe we could come out of this not only triumphant—but *together*.

Chapter Twelve

Claude promptly ruined my hopeful mood.

"I'm almost glad that you overheard them, because it lightens my load to know that Luc is innocent. But then, everything is worse. Because they know you're helping me. Even if they didn't see you, they know because I took you to that witch's den. I'm so sorry, Beatrice."

My guilt that had been building since he'd knocked on my door suddenly needed an outlet. He believed his friend to be innocent, and I hated to make things harder for him, to make him question his place in the world. But he had to know.

He pulled me in close and nuzzled my neck, threatening to distract me. But I couldn't let him.

"I've seen Luc before. In a vision. I'm sorry, Claude, but he isn't innocent."

He stilled in my arms. "What did you see?"

Out with it all. I was literally naked in his arms. Might as well be emotionally naked, too.

"My brother Eddie disappeared when I was ten years old. He was older, nineteen. We—we never had the chance to become close, you know? And I've always wondered if we would have been—if we'd had the chance."

"I remember you mentioning him before. What happened to him?"

I shrugged, and he stepped back and helped me hop off the table. Underwear. Surely I had underwear somewhere around here.

"He disappeared. His body was never found. No information other than part of his jacket found on a street corner known for drug dealing. Some blood at the scene came back as his."

Ah-ha. My underwear. I dressed quickly, but Claude didn't worry about his shirt. I did my best not to let my eyes roam over his hard chest. I couldn't afford for either of us to be distracted right now, not until I'd gotten all this out.

"And you saw Luc? That is...difficult to believe." His joking tone returned. "Perhaps you think all us vampires look alike?"

I tugged my shirt over my head and met Claude's guarded expression on the other side. He might wear the grin of a man unaffected, but he wasn't as nonchalant as he wanted to appear.

"The detective came by so my parents could identify the piece of jacket. He took it out of the bag and set it on top. My mother was—well, she was upset. Both of my parents were. They left the room. The detective followed." My voice sounded hollow to my own ears. Shouldn't I feel something sharper? But I didn't. I just felt numb recounting the story that had changed my life.

"Leaving you alone with the fabric."

"Yes."

"Getting a vision so young would be...unusual."

Unlikely. Near impossible. That's what he meant, but I silently thanked him for his word choice. "My parents thought—everyone thought—that it was just my imagination. That I had a nightmare that was so realistic it made me think it had actually happened. The nightmare part was true, it reoccurred for years after his actual disappearance. And I eventually convinced myself that was the real order of things. That I'd had a nightmare about my brother being attacked, and that it was so vivid I got confused." I took a deep breath at the thought of the nightmares. "But it was a vision that caused the nightmares."

"What did you see?"

"I saw Luc, smiling. I saw his fangs flash. A dark car. I felt Eddie's pain."

"That is all?"

A rush of anger overtook my numbness. "It was enough," I growled.

He came to me and pulled me into a tight hug. I leaned against him, breathing his scent, for a brief moment allowing myself to relax.

"I convinced myself that it was just a nightmare. And it made sense. I didn't show any signs of psychometry again until after high school. I took a standard test when I enrolled in the police academy. The OWEA wasn't far behind. My lack of a college degree didn't even slow down their offer when my results came back." I laughed, but it was halfhearted at best. "You should have seen my parents' reaction. They didn't even realize it ran in our family."

"It isn't always active in those who carry the gene."

"Or it's too weak for them to ever notice." I shrugged. "Either way, they weren't pleased. Then again, they haven't been pleased by too much since my brother—" I shook my head. What was the use in dwelling on the past, on things I couldn't change? Not much.

His hand slid down my arm and I fought the urge to step back into the safety of his embrace.

"My brother wasn't an angel. He had been into some bad things before he disappeared. We were poor, and he wasn't happy about it. He...wasn't averse to making money however he needed to." Dealing drugs. Who knew what else? For someone so young, he'd gotten himself into a lot of trouble. "But whatever he did, he didn't deserve to just disappear like that."

"Have you looked into his case? Since joining the OWEA?"

"Nope." And it had taken every bit of my willpower and self-control not to at times, while at other moments I felt ill at even the thought of looking in that file. It was a Pandora's box, ready to shit all over the bit of a life I'd built. Once opened, I'd never be able to close it.

"Perhaps we should speak to Luc about this."

"You don't believe me." Something in my chest twisted. I hadn't expected him to believe me—not exactly. But it would have been nice to be surprised for once.

"It's not that. I just—"

"Need more evidence than my word. I got it."

"Beatrice." He slid his hand under my chin and tipped it so I would meet his gaze. "I'm so sorry for the loss of your brother. I believe that you believe what you saw was real, and was Luc. I do not doubt your word. But, the memories from childhood…they're so easy to alter in our own minds even as we seek clarity. They're shadows of reality. I'd hate to condemn a man I trust based on such memories."

He was right. But everything in my being insisted that Luc was in the vision I'd seen as a child. And his presence in the vision from the brand hadn't yet been explained either. Even though it was starting to look more like Nicolas was responsible for that crime.

"I know what I saw." There was nothing else to say but that, although I didn't have anything concrete to argue with. Frustration and helplessness rolled through me, and must have shown in my expression, because Claude stepped toward me again.

"I'm more worried that they may have seen you. If Nicolas believes you overheard them…" He shook his head. "I can't let him hurt you, *mon amour*."

I didn't know what to say to that. I didn't even know how to feel. My gut twisted and my pulse raced. Happiness that he cared warred with fear at the resignation in his voice.

"Maybe you should finish getting dressed." I stepped away. I couldn't be so close to him right now and still think straight.

He laughed softly. "All right. I will get dressed. We will sleep. And tomorrow, we will do what needs to be done."

He'd said we. *We would do what needed to be done.* But he'd meant I. That much was obvious when I awoke alone the next morning. I called his name once, but the silence in the condo was oppressive.

"Fucking idiot," I muttered. He'd left a note by the coffeepot. Basic, but gut-wrenching all the same. Let him take care of his problem. Couldn't let anyone else be hurt. Blah blah blah… We'd do dinner.

He was a stupid, heroic vampire. An irreplaceable man. And he was walking into a trap.

Even on the off chance Nicolas didn't expect him. Wasn't planning on him showing up to protect me or seek justice. It didn't matter. Nicolas wouldn't be alone. As the son of a Magister and powerful vampire in his own right, he'd have handlers or bodyguards or a few fucking yes men to help him off Claude. And Claude was going in with a dangerous assumption: that Luc's loyalties were with him, not with his own son.

I couldn't let that happen.

He might hate me for it, might consider it a betrayal, but I had to go to the police.

I dressed quickly and decided to go to Chicago's Paranormal Unit. My words would carry more weight with the Otherworlder Enforcement Agency, but Chicago's freak squad was better staffed than the local OWEA branch. And they had more reason to give a shit about Claude. I considered calling, but the situation was too complex, too difficult to explain over the telephone. It would be simpler, and quicker, in person.

As if affected by my mood, gray clouds hung heavily over the city, and the oppressive cold sank through my coat and scarf almost immediately. I looked down the street for a cab. There. I raised my hand to wave, and a sharp pain stabbed the back of my neck. Someone pulled me against his body. I could see and hear the rush of the wind, but I couldn't move my head to see who held me. My mouth wouldn't work. Panic roared through me, but I couldn't cry out. Couldn't fight back.

The gloved arm pulled me into a car, and finally I caught a glimpse of the man's face. The man who was kidnapping me.

Luc Chevalier. The Magister.

Frustration fought against the panic as we pulled away from the curb. I was lain across the backseat of the vehicle, my legs across Luc's lap. I couldn't see the driver. Dark tinted windows hid us from the rest of the world. For a brief moment, I had the insane idea that they couldn't see me. That I wasn't really there. That I was instead locked into someone else's vision. An idea that Luc quickly shattered.

"I apologize for the spell, Miss Davis. You'll understand that we couldn't have you calling out for help or hurting yourself trying to get away."

The vampire's voice was smooth, placating. The voice of a politician.

"You won't be harmed. You have my word."

Right. Totally a politician. I could see why the vampires followed him. I almost believed him when he said I wouldn't be harmed. I wanted to believe him. But, I also wasn't an idiot. People weren't kidnapped, allowed to see their kidnappers, and then simply released. It just didn't happen.

Panic rose in me again at the thought, and I pushed it down as best I could and tried to think my way through the situation. I still couldn't move. But chances were, if this was a basic disabling spell Luc commissioned, I would be immobilized for less than an hour. Surely it would take longer than that for them to take me somewhere to kill me, or whatever they had planned for me first. I'd get my chance then.

But what kind of chance would I have?

Luc was one of the strongest vampires in the country, and definitely on the shortlist for the most powerful in the world. Sure, there were probably a few who could take him out in Europe and Asia where the older families lived, but I didn't have an ancient vampire handy, so fighting my way free wasn't an option.

I'd have to run. Or scream. Possibly run away screaming.

Awesome plan.

Luc didn't say anything else, and we rode silently for a while. Finally, a tingle started in my fingertips. The spell was wearing off—and by my estimate we'd been driving nearly an hour. If I had to, maybe I could surprise them. Jump out of the car when it slowed. Bruises and broken bones were better than being dead.

Before I could contemplate how best to roll when I hit the ground, the car slowed and the light outside the windows dimmed. The car engine ceased its rumble, and Luc opened the door. We'd arrived, wherever it was we were going.

Luc pulled me out of the car carefully, then carried me as if I were a bride, across the threshold into a house. The smell of cigarettes touched my nose, but I couldn't be sure if it was the house, or someone walking in front of us. A cottage-cheese ceiling was all I could make out from my vantage point, and I frowned. No way were we at the Magister's house. The vampire just didn't strike me as the type to have 1980s popcorn ceilings anywhere on his property.

My arm twitched of its own volition and Luc made an approving noise.

"Good. You'll be able to move normally in a minute or two. That'll make this easier."

We emerged from the hallway, and the smell of old cigarettes filled my nose. Oh yes, it was the house that stank. Whoever lived here wasn't worried about cracking a window for a smoke. Luc lay me down on a couch, gentle again. If he really intended to kill me, would he be so careful not to hurt me now?

A door slammed in another room. A loud thump, like an exterior door, but not from the same direction we'd entered. The light sound of footsteps approaching. My heart jumped into my throat. Another vampire? Why the hell not? I could handle three as well as two—meaning not at all.

"What the hell did you do to her?" The voice was familiar and, even across the room, sent hope rushing through me. But the hope was quickly stamped out by dread.

Claude was here. But so was Luc and who knew how many vampires?

What chance did we have?

"It's a simple disabling spell. She's otherwise unharmed."

Movement in the corner of my eye made me start, and to my surprise, my body actually twitched.

"Jesus, Luc. I could have picked her up. This wasn't necessary." Footsteps against carpet, then, "Can you move, Beatrice?" Claude's voice was low and soothing, and only inches from my ear. "Try to move."

It took a couple of minutes, but with some concentrated effort and a whole lot of built up fear and anger, I was able to work myself up into a sitting position.

"…Fucker," I finally managed once I could speak again.

Luc offered me a small, apologetic smile. "I understand why you would be upset. But we needed to speak to you without making a scene. And Claude was otherwise detained."

"I was checking on the capture of a rogue witch—one your son is well-acquainted with. You could have given me more than fifteen minutes to return your phone call," Claude growled.

"I'm afraid time was of the essence."

"Could've…asked." Forming words was still a challenge. Like I'd been tossed in a deep freeze and was trying to thaw my muscles. Thankfully minus the cold.

The room revealed by my sitting position wasn't much better than the smell. The couch I sat on was old and frayed, and a stack of beer bottles sat on the coffee table next to a full ashtray. It looked—and smelled—like a bachelor pad of a college-aged boy who'd decided to party his early twenties away instead of actually going to college.

"You'll understand if I didn't think you'd be likely to trust me, considering my presence in your visions," Luc said, and the man behind him who stood in the shadows shifted almost imperceptibly. Only two of them, then—Luc and the driver? Fewer than I would have guessed if he was looking for a fight.

Luc's words sank in, and my gaze shot to Claude. Sure enough, he glanced down. Guilt covered his expression.

"You told him? My great big secret I only just confided in you? How long did you wait, Claude? Did you call him last night, or did you wait to slither out of bed this morning to do it?" Betrayed. By Claude. I couldn't even grasp the emotions washing through me. Anger and fear and such an overwhelming sadness that I had to choke down tears.

Overrunning it all was exhaustion.

Why the hell had I crawled out of my comfortable bed, my safe life, to help this man? To crack open my past that would have been just fine staying where it was. In the past.

"I'm giving him a chance to explain. He's an honorable man." Claude turned to Luc, his brows pinched in annoyance. "I didn't think he'd spell you and bring you here. And I'm still not clear why we're meeting in this place."

"It's a good thing he trusted me, Miss Davis."

"*Agent* Davis." I faced Luc and the rage started to win. "A good thing? I saw your face, Luc. I know you were there when my brother was killed."

Forcing myself to my feet, I struggled for balance. I couldn't face this man sitting down.

"I've seen your face in my nightmares, *Magister*." I spit his title with as much venom as I could manage. "You've haunted my flights since I was ten."

A muscle in Luc's jaw twitched, but he didn't otherwise show any outward emotion.

"Listen to him, *mon chou*."

I whirled on Claude, catching myself with the corner of the couch's armrest before I could topple over and ruin any chance I had of being taken seriously. "Don't call me that. You just lost that right."

Claude flinched as if I'd hit him with my fist instead of my words. "Please. Just listen."

Guilt hit me at his words, his pained expression. He'd done what he thought was right. Was his decision so much different than my own when I'd decided to get the police department involved? Not really. Biggest difference was, I hadn't had the chance to betray his secret.

"I know that the last thing you want to hear is the sound of my voice, Agent Davis, so I'll be quick. I was there when your brother disappeared. But I didn't kill him."

I narrowed my eyes at the vampire. "Bullshit. Visions are related to emotion. He would have seen you as the most important thing in the room for your face to imprint onto his clothing. And it would have had to have been during a heck of a traumatic event."

"I might have been the most important thing to him in that moment. But it's not because I killed him." Luc's eyes revealed an iron will, and I could see why he'd ruled his small part of the world for so long. But I was beyond fear of this vampire. I'd lived my life afraid of him, of what he represented, even when I'd just thought him a nightmare. I was done being afraid.

"Oh, really. Then why the hell would your face be the first thing I saw?"

"It's because I saved his life. Your brother, Agent Davis, is not dead."

Chapter Thirteen

"You're a liar." If the Magister had physically punched me in the gut, I didn't think it would have hurt as much as the twisting pain that struck me with his words.

I started to turn to look at Claude, but movement behind the Magister drew my eyes back. The man who had been hovering behind the Magister stepped out of the shadows, and all the air left the room.

The fine line of his jaw was the same, as was the carrot-colored hair and pale skin. His hair hadn't darkened into a true red like mine; it had stayed lighter. But he looked smaller somehow. The young man I remembered had always seemed so large.

But then, he would have seemed so to a ten-year-old.

The young man in front of me, tentative smile on his face, was of average height and slight build. And more important, he was a *young* man.

My brother had been nine years my senior when he

disappeared. I had been ten. The man in front of me hadn't aged a day since—he looked every bit nineteen years old.

"Vampire." My voice was barely perceptible to my ears, but vampires had great hearing. Mind reeling, I couldn't for the life of me get it to stop. Couldn't come up with a single thought other than that word.

"Your brother was injured that night. Gravely. I saved his life and made him a vampire—against vampire law, I should point out. I've had to pay dearly for it, but I'd do it again. No doubt that was a powerful enough event to imprint his coat."

Something about that wasn't right, but I couldn't grasp it. But Claude wasn't as affected.

"A grave injury cured by a vampire turning? Sounds like he was bitten. Another *mistake* of Nicolas's?"

I couldn't for the life of me tear my gaze from my brother Eddie's face to look at Claude, but I could hear the growl in his voice. The anger.

"Is there ever going to come a time when you realize his harmless mistakes are anything but?" Claude asked.

Luc smiled bitterly, and the vampire behind him—my brother—shifted on his feet. "As you can see, your brother is alive and well. We're in his house, in fact. He is not being held prisoner, nor is he being coerced."

I could see that, but that created more questions in my mind than it answered.

"Why didn't—" I shook my head, and it was as if pieces of a puzzle settled, each fitting into its rightful place. Anger settled into my chest, smothering any affection. I glared at my brother, hard. If looks could have killed, he would have dropped right then and there. "You just took off for a new life and left the old one because you didn't give a shit, didn't you?"

I wanted him to argue the fact. I wanted him to say he was coerced or had amnesia or was locked in a dungeon. I wanted him to tell me that my memory was faulty, that he hadn't been as unhappy with his lot in life as I remembered. That he hadn't constantly argued with our parents. That he hadn't just left without a word.

But he just shrugged. "I gave a shit. Hell, I missed you, Bea. But you know how they were to me."

His words sounded hollow, and the whiny, self-entitled tone I'd heard from my teenage brother was still there in this pseudo-man. He'd missed me the way he might miss a favorite record. Not like he should have missed a family member. Had being made a perpetual teenager kept his attitudes the same as the truculent kid he'd been back then, or would he never have grown up, even if he'd been given the chance?

"Since your brother is quite alive, I beseech you both to let go of this needless investigation into my family."

That would be so much easier. And in fact, I ached to leave this whole mess behind me. Leave Eddie behind me. Leave all these damn vampires to their business. Even Claude. Especially Claude. To go and find a life that didn't involve vampires of any sort. To pretend my brother died that night—or hell, maybe reach out to him to figure out if he might potentially grow into a good man.

But Claude—Claude had worked to bring Nic to justice for years. Maybe decades. Probably longer than I'd been alive.

And despite the fact that he had blabbed my secret to a man I considered an enemy, I realized that I *loved* the misguided vampire. Enough to put myself on the line to help him bring his obsession to a close.

"Blood isn't everything. A man as old as you should know that. Your son deserves to rot in prison—or worse. And as far as I'm concerned, you do, too. Go fuck yourself," I told Luc. I nodded to my brother—how little he deserved that title. "And you can go fuck yourself, too."

Luc, resignation in his posture, turned to Claude, who said, "I'm with her. He has to be stopped, Luc. I know that you don't want to believe him truly evil. I know you want to attribute his actions to simple rash decisions—to emotional outbursts. But he will continue to hurt people. And I just can't allow it. Not any longer."

As if a light switch had been clicked, Luc suddenly looked every bit the ancient vampire—the old man—that he was. His perfect skin didn't wrinkle, neither did his hairline recede or his muscles fade. But he looked exhausted, and resigned. He nodded slowly, as if the gesture pained him. "Nicolas warned me that you would not bend on this. I'd hoped that I could convince you."

"Nicolas knows of this?"

"I didn't tell him I was coming here, talking to you and the agent, if that's what you're asking." I half expected Luc to attack, but he simply stood a moment.

"You've been helping him." Claude's voice lost all of its anger. He sounded let down. "You were there when he used the brand to mark that selkie. Just as you were there when Beatrice's brother was almost killed."

Becoming the topic of conversation didn't agree with my brother. He fidgeted when Claude's gaze slid to him, and glanced nervously at the front door behind me as if he wanted to run away.

"Of course I was there," Luc said. "I am present for all of my son's sins. I clean them up. I punish him. And I pray that they will not be repeated. But I am never without sorrow. Never without regret."

"Fuck your regret," Claude said, and finally some fire returned to his voice. "You've enabled this. You've covered up for him for what? A century? More? I can't let this stand, and I can no longer wait for your permission or your judgment."

"I know you can't. But I promised *her*. I swore to always keep him safe." He struggled for his words. "I couldn't keep her alive, Claude. But I swore that I would do better for our son."

Claude took a step forward and Eddie jumped, just a little bit. He looked at the door again. Damn. Was Claude really that scary, or was my brother that much of a wimp?

"I can't pretend to forgive what you have done—no matter how good you thought your reason. Where will you stand now?"

"I cannot help you in this, you know that."

"But you've already taken a stand, haven't you? That's why I'm out of town so much now, sent to handle affairs that you used to handle."

"Not exactly." Luc shook his head. "I needed to be here—to stop him—"

"To clean up his messes, or to keep me from catching him with the evidence you couldn't refute?" Claude's fists clenched and unclenched at his side, but his words came out calm. "Very well, *maître*."

No. That was far too accepting for my taste. The Magister might get away with siding with his son—I could understand that, even if I couldn't contemplate ever making such a decision myself. But for Claude to stand neutral?

I opened my mouth to give him a piece of my mind, but never got the words out. My brother flinched behind Luc.

I barely had time to duck in front of the couch when the door burst open and a vampire sprinted in so quickly I registered the door opening after the vampire was nearly on Claude.

A shot rang out. Claude. He'd pulled and fired so swiftly at the vampire approaching, I hadn't even seen it.

The vamp barely slowed. Long knife in hand, he stabbed at Claude. I almost couldn't wrap my mind around it, even though I knew that a bullet wouldn't do much damage to a vampire.

The vampire hit Claude and they fell into a dance too fast for me to follow. Claude fired again, slowing his opponent a hair. Then the gun flew, through the doorway and into the kitchen beyond. I almost went after it before reality hit. I wouldn't just have to get through the vampire fighting Claude—not to mention I'd be hopeless at navigating around their fast, brutal fight—but I'd have to get past Luc, too.

Movement drew my gaze back to the door, where another vampire followed in the first's wake. Him, I got a good look at. Because he didn't bother to run in at vampire speed. He sauntered in after the other vamp broke the door off its hinges. And he was carrying a freaking sword.

Nicolas Chevalier.

I vaguely wondered if the neighbors would be calling the police.

If there were any neighbors. Were we in a city? Out in the middle of nowhere? No way to tell from inside the house.

Luc watched as Claude wrestled with one vampire, fighting for the knife, and Nic closed in behind them. My heart jumped into my throat at the sight of that knife. Vampires were tough to kill, but not impossible. Take out the heart or the head. And it was a big freaking knife.

My brother backed up a step, looking unsure. I felt uselessly for my sidearm. What the fuck kind of help could I be without a gun? The vampires seemed to think the same, because their focus was entirely on Claude.

My answer stared at me in the face. The coffee table.

No chance of hitting the vampire Claude fought with; they moved at speeds that hurt my eyes. No chance to get past all of them to Claude's nearly useless gun. But Nicolas. Arrogant, prodigal son, he was watching his lackey fight Claude—weakening him for the kill.

A kill that Nicolas's gleeful expression left little doubt that he'd participate in. I had faith that Claude could take out the vampire he wrestled with. And Luc and my brother might stay out of the fight—until things looked bad for them, anyway.

Hell. My brother. No wonder he'd been watching the door so nervously. He'd known they were coming. He'd betrayed me—us—to Nicolas. The man who'd almost killed him. What had Nicolas said or done to bring him around. Offered him money?

My chest hurt at the thought. Shit. Sure, he hadn't always made the right choices in his life. But to betray me to someone he had to know intended to kill me? I couldn't accept that.

I pushed up from the ground and grabbed the coffee table. Cheap and light, parts of the wood covering had rubbed or ripped away to reveal the particleboard beneath. It practically screamed Ikea. But it was a simple model. Helpful if you didn't have super strength.

I used my whole body when I threw it at Nicolas. I knew it wouldn't hurt him, but for Claude to survive, I needed to keep his attention. Claude was my only hope.

And I was his.

Nicolas reacted immediately to my attack. The vampire flew at me, and I didn't even see him move until he was on top of me. The idea of a vampire other than Claude biting me sickened me. Between us, it was personal. It was about trust. It was intimate. A show of love.

But Nicolas didn't bite me. *He threw me.*

I hit the wall and for a moment I felt like I was in a vision. Sound disappeared. I couldn't move. Shock halted my thoughts.

Then it all came rushing back. I sucked in a breath of air and sharp pain spiked from the back of my ribs where I'd hit the wall. I slid down the surface of the wood paneling to the floor.

Across the room, Claude stood facing me, facing Nicolas. The Magister's son seemed to have decided I was no longer a threat, because he turned his back to me and faced off with Claude.

The vampire Claude had been wrestling with was crumpled into an unmoving pile at Claude's feet. Claude held the vampire's bloody knife. There was so much blood. On the vampire. On the floor. On Claude's hands.

But others were there now. Two more vampires had come in at some point and, based on their proximity to Nicolas, I didn't think they were there to help us.

Like a light snuffed, the bit of hope I'd nursed that we'd make it out of this died at the sight of them. There were too many.

Luc was shouting something but, like in my visions, I couldn't seem to grasp what he said. His expression had turned dark, his eyes narrowed in worry, and he gestured at Nic and Claude.

I struggled to my feet, fighting against the pain spiking from my back. Something was wrong with my left shoulder, and my arm didn't want to move. But my right arm worked just fine, and I would be damned if I didn't at least go out fighting.

The two vampires who'd entered while I was on the floor circled Claude, and he kept them at bay with the knife and a fearsomely calm expression. Nicolas stood watching, his back to me. I'd been right. The man didn't like to risk himself when he wasn't certain of the result. That was okay. I really wanted to hit him, anyway.

The lamp fell off the end table when I grabbed the leg. I swung it like a club, hitting Nicolas. It didn't break under the strength of only one of my arms swinging it so haphazardly, but bounced off his back, instead.

But it got his attention.

"Asshole!" I yelled when he turned.

"You'll pay for that," he growled.

"Probably. But you're still an ass."

Then I was hitting the wall again, but this time the vampire was attached to my throat. In the distance, I could see Claude cry out to me and, seeing an opening, the vampires circling him attacked.

Pain arched through my body from my throat, and I

batted at Nicolas with my working arm. He pressed so hard against my neck that I couldn't breathe right. Then everything slowed down, and an almost pleasant fuzzy haze covered the scene before me.

Nicolas lifted his head and grinned, my blood covering his mouth and chin.

"Messy eater," I muttered, or tried to. The words came out garbled.

Nicolas turned to shout over his shoulder. "You should have minded your own business, Claude. This is your fault. You got her killed!"

Claude screamed back something nonsensical and one of the vampires on top of him flew out the bay window.

Nicolas turned back to me. "Let's get this over with, shall we? I do like to play with my food, but you're a little bland."

He started toward my neck again, then fell back a couple of steps. I fell to the ground, right on my butt. My legs didn't seem to work. And for a moment, I thought I'd passed out and gone to dreamland.

My brother stood between Nicolas and me.

"She can't do anything to you. Leave her be," he said.

It wasn't a resounding defense, but the fact he stood between us was enough. More than I would have expected. Maybe not enough to forgive everything, but it got him closer.

Nicolas looked like he might acquiesce for a moment, his gaze flashing between me and Eddie. Then he grinned, and struck.

My brother hit the wall next to me, and slid into a puddle beside me. Knocked out or dead? I couldn't tell.

My neck was wet and I was starting to get cold. And at

any moment, Nicolas would be on me, finishing his goal of bleeding me dry.

But Nicolas never hit me. Instead, I watched him turn to his father.

"What did you say to me?" Nicolas asked.

"I said leave the woman alone." Luc's graying pallor and the almost crazy look in his eyes made me hope that Nicolas had finally pushed his father too far. "This has gone far enough, my son."

I couldn't see Nicolas's expression, but I could hear the smile in his voice. "You're right, father. This has gone far enough, and for long enough. The pieces are all in place. And here you are, all alone."

Nicolas was blocking my view of Claude. Was he hurt? Dead? God, I had to see. Limbs screaming and head spinning, I tried to force myself up into a standing position. When a wave of blackness stole seconds from me I decided, instead, to crawl but I shuffled on my knees because I only had one good arm.

Nicolas jumped at his father, and I could see the other vampire Claude had been fighting jump Luc as well. But I didn't care about them. I had to see if Claude was okay. I had to see if my brother was okay.

He wasn't.

I shuffled a couple of feet to look at Eddie. His face was bleeding, his nose broken. Maybe his jaw. But it took more than that to kill a vampire. Even with blood seeping out of the back of his head, right? I knew that young ones were easier to kill, but surely not head-injury easy. I hoped.

I touched the side of his face, as if touching him would make him being here real, and my hand slid down to his shirt. That's when I saw it.

His shirt had opened just enough—courtesy of a broken button—for the brand on his chest to be visible.

Shit.

Nic and Luc continued to fight, and a piece of the couch hit the drywall above my head. I ducked and closed my eyes, but it landed a foot behind me. I turned back to my brother.

Did Nic have a hold on him, too? Is that why he'd told the vampire we'd be here with Luc? What the fuck did the brand do? Not torture people, that was for sure. If that had been the case, then the giant wouldn't have given that up.

But *controlling* someone from a distance would fit. If I were the giant, I would've tried to keep the lie as close to the truth as possible. That way he could feign ignorance if Claude caught on.

What could Nic possibly gain from branding someone like my brother and a selkie leader? They had nothing in common.

Unless…unless Nic used the brand to control them somehow. That would fit. A selkie prince would be useful—not on his own, but if Nic was making a big move to take over. Hell, was it possible he controlled people using the brand as a link?

I didn't know, and I wasn't entirely sure it mattered. Right now, we had to survive.

I only made it a couple of feet, just far enough to see Claude on the floor, unmoving. Pain the likes of which I never thought I could feel clawed at my insides, and I finally gave up on my fight to move. I curled up on the floor. I couldn't cry. I couldn't scream. I couldn't allow the darkness I so craved to pull me under.

Because I was stronger than that. And Claude would expect more of me. I reached out and grabbed a chunk of wood that was next to me on the floor. From the coffee table, maybe. And I held it in my hands, waiting for Nicolas to attack.

Somehow, I knew that Nicolas would win. Luc hadn't been able to bring his son to heel for more than a century, and taking his son's life would be a far greater step than that. But Luc's sense of honor wouldn't allow him to watch his friend die without at least attempting to stop it either. Luc didn't plan on surviving.

I closed my eyes, still clinging to my bit of wood. The scuffle continued, far more quietly than I would have guessed. Not much yelling. No cursing or one-liners. No insults. Just the sound of flesh hitting flesh, of knives clattering to the floor. The occasional boom of someone hitting a wall. Amazingly, nothing hit me.

The room was so cold, and I was so fucking tired. Blood loss, part of my brain insisted. A short nap, a little rest, maybe then I could get up.

No.

I forced my eyes open. The hell I was going to let some asshole vampire kill me while I lay unconscious. I struggled to my knees, using my right hand to prop myself up, my small wannabe stake between my hand and the ground. I couldn't let it go, even though I knew if I tried to use it, I'd face-plant into the ground the second I lifted my hand from where it propped me up.

Blinking at the scene before me, I tried to take it in. Nicolas stood in front of his father, their profiles to me. Pieces of what could only be the other vampires were on the ground. They were both covered in blood and beat the hell up. But when Luc's gaze slid to me, he moved just enough so I could see his chest. And the long sword that stuck out from where his heart should've been.

He mouthed something to me. It might have been, "I'm sorry."

Then Nic turned around.

Nothing sane dwelt in him—not really. I'd have sworn to it at that moment, staring into those eyes so full of hate.

"It's my turn now. No one to order me around. No one to try to make me live within the bounds of human law." His expression twisted into a snarl so fierce he looked inhuman. "We're better than you! Why did he always try to protect you?"

He lunged toward me, and I couldn't help but cry out when he bent to take my neck again. He paused for a moment, lips so close to the skin on my neck that I could feel the rush from his mouth when he laughed. I cringed, then with my last bit of strength, I plunged my wannabe stake into his stomach.

He laughed louder and pulled back, wheezing as he chortled. He plucked the wood from his stomach and tossed it. He leaned in again, and I silently prayed that Claude might still be alive. That he might get away. That Eddie might get away with him.

But before Nicolas's teeth could break my skin, his body stiffened. Something hit my chest—cooler than my skin but warmer than the air around us. A full second passed before I registered the knifepoint sticking out from his chest. And that what had hit me was his blood.

Claude knocked Nicolas to the side, moving him away

from me.

Hope surged through me. If Nicolas was dead, we were saved. I was so fucking cold, and Claude was torn up—covered in blood and his body nearly broken by the vampires he'd fought. But if there was no one left to fight, we had a chance.

I blinked against the darkness that crept into the edges of my vision, and movement caught my eye. Nicolas was moving. Slowly, but moving. Headed for the door.

Had Claude missed the heart?

"Get him," I muttered, but Claude didn't move from my side. I wasn't sure it mattered. I wasn't so cold anymore, but I was so fucking tired.

"I'm not leaving you."

"You've…fought so…long." Words didn't seem to want to form in my mouth, and I wondered if one of the vampire hits had knocked my jaw out of whack. But it didn't hurt.

"He doesn't matter." Claude didn't even glance at Nic, who had struggled to his feet. "I need you to make a choice, *mon chou*. Will you stay with me?"

His question seemed to have deeper meaning than I could grasp in that moment. But the idea of being with him—trusting him not to hurt me—didn't scare me anymore. He loved me. I loved him. It all seemed so damned simple now. There was no need to deny it anymore.

"Love…you," I managed.

Claude was cursing then, and I realized he'd been talking and I missed it. He shoved something against my mouth and I fought him instinctually. But even in his beaten state, the vampire was a good deal stronger than I.

Sweet coppery heat filled my mouth. I gagged and

coughed into his arm, but he didn't move. I managed to swallow, but the liquid kept coming. I thought I passed out for a second, but the blood flow never seemed to stop. My stomach felt horrible, like I desperately needed to vomit. If I could just move. But I couldn't move. Claude was yelling at me, telling me to drink. Telling me not to die. Not yet.

If he was desperately trying to fill my body with his blood, then I had to be dying. Because vampires weren't made without human death.

Heat rolled through my stomach and spread to the rest of me. It was painful compared to the cold I'd been feeling, and awakened all the pain from my injuries. I tried to cry out, but I couldn't put a voice to the agony. I couldn't find a release for the heat building. Every part of my body throbbed.

Over Claude's arm, something moved. Luc came into view, his eyes on us and his expression unreadable. With one quick jerk, he pulled the sword from his chest.

The world went blessedly dark.

Chapter Fourteen

The fishy smell of the ocean filled my lungs. Waves rolled, hitting the beach in front of me, then sliding back out. To my ears, it sounded like the roar of a helicopter—close and likely to hit me if I didn't duck. That part was supposed to get better.

My stomach twisted, and I was hit by a sudden hunger. One that I didn't have to feed, not yet, but which I craved more than just about anything I could remember. That part was supposed to get better, too, but it would never go away.

Such was the price I had paid.

And I had paid with my gift. Psychometry wasn't a talent vampires possessed. I had lost my visions. My ability to witness murders after the fact. My occasional ability to glimpse the future. That was something that would have killed me a week ago, would have made me feel entirely worthless. But now, the idea made me almost giddy, if a touch sad, when I let myself dwell on the loss.

"Getting melancholy on me, out here staring at the waves?"

I smiled but didn't turn around. "Just enjoying the view."

"You're not missing the Midwest winter are you? Because I have a cabin in North Dakota that would provide the seclusion we need for you to adjust. It's not Chicago, but it'll do if you'd prefer the cold we left behind."

I shivered. Just the thought of the freezing Chicago wind was enough to make me never want to leave this small island. I wasn't sure exactly where we were—I hadn't asked—but it was warm here, humid. The beaches were beautiful. And we were the only people on the island.

That was good enough for me.

"Don't you dare threaten me with cold, mister." I turned and poked Claude in the chest. "Them's fightin' words. And they'll get you bit."

He grinned and pulled me close for a quick kiss, but worry flashed in his eyes. I didn't bother calling him on it. He'd eventually figure out that I wasn't going to slip into a great depression because he'd been forced to choose between watching me die or turning me into a so-called creature of the night.

I was glad he'd chosen the way he had. And someday he'd believe it, too. We had plenty of time. It had only been a week, after all.

"Got a call from Lieutenant Vasquez."

"Your supervisor?"

"Yes. He wasn't too happy with me leaving him and the rest of the unit with the cleanup. That many dead vampires—well, there's a lot of paperwork."

"I'll bet." I'd been unconscious for the day after the

events had unfolded in my brother's rural home. And I'd been practically a zombie for days after that—nearly a literal one. Thinking much beyond the hunger for blood had been impossible. And the heat that had roiled through me from Claude's blood hadn't faded for several days—after I'd died from my injuries, to be reborn as a vampire.

I tried not to think about that part too closely.

My memories were sketchy, but Claude had filled in the details. He'd let Nic go to save me—I remembered that much. But Luc, after making sure I would live, had found Nic on the front steps. He'd been nearly dead from the blow to his heart that Claude had inflicted with the sword, but Luc had cut off his head, just to be sure.

It seemed that the father had finally run out of patience with his son.

Before the police and paramedics had arrived, Luc and Eddie had left. I hoped that meant my brother still lived. And that somewhere, Luc was looking out for him.

"I might have to fly back to Chicago for a few days, but I told him we needed some time here. OWEA is stepping in to help close out the case. But without Nic—or Luc—burying things, evidence is piling up. Vasquez is willing to interview you over the phone until you're up to meeting with him."

I could do that much. Things were getting easier to deal with than they had been, and with each passing day my strange new world was starting to feel more normal, more natural. Surely I could manage a phone call. In fact, I could manage a few. I needed to call my parents and talk to them personally, instead of through Claude.

"Evidence," I muttered. It was strange. Words felt different coming out of my mouth as a vampire. As if everything had a taste. I turned back to the ocean. "I will get used to this, right?"

He pulled me close, his hard chest against my back, and his arms cradling me. "You will."

"So what's the evidence saying?"

"Are you sure you want to talk about this now?" he murmured, mouth close to my ear, his face pressed against my hair.

"I'm still an investigator. Or I will be, once I get a handle on this new B.S." Like my new overwhelming desire for blood. *Shit*.

No. I couldn't get freaked out. Claude said it would get better, and I believed him.

"It seems like we were right. Nic's been building power. The brands that the giant told us were for torture—well, not quite. He bent the truth. An OWEA-hired shaman, with Natalie's help, was able to figure that out. They did connect Nic to the selkie prince and others. But it didn't allow for torture, it was to control them. Get them to do things at key times. Others he had blackmail material on, and I'm sure he had a couple of otherworlder leaders he was going to bribe. He had planned to take over his father's territory. And given Nic's narcissism and his stash of power, I'm sure that was just the first step."

It was as I'd thought, as I'd lain there on the floor, waiting to die. "I wonder why he marked my brother."

"Several of the vamps were marked. Just enough to en- sure that Nic had some loyal to him when the coup came. Crazy though. The amount of power he would have had to harness to be able to control that many people would have been tremendous. I don't know if he planned on only activating the brand on one or two at a time when he needed them, or if he planned something really horrible to drum up enough power to be able to control more."

"Anything on the shaman who helped him?"

"Nothing yet. But with the resources the OWEA and Chicago PD are putting behind this, they'll find him." He took a haggard breath. "I'm still shocked that Luc knew—really knew. That he was sending me away as much as he could to try to bring Nic to heel. But all he did was give Nic more opportunity to build his resources."

"He loved his son." And the whole family was off their rockers. But I didn't say that. Out of respect for Claude. And out of a weird understanding for Luc. Even given everything he'd done—and perhaps more important, the things he hadn't—the man hadn't wanted to see people hurt.

"He was desperate. And selfish," Claude said.

Truth. Not the whole of it, but it was true enough.

Claude nuzzled my neck. "Let's talk of more pleasant things."

I couldn't help smiling again. I was doing a lot of that lately—smiling. Far too much for a person who had been near death a week ago, and who was still nursing wounds from the experience. But maybe that was the trick. The threat of everything being taken away gave me a new appreciation for it all.

"What would you like to talk about?"

"Us."

I smiled. That was fine by me. There was an "us" now. And it was something we could have for a very long time. Forever.

Acknowledgments

There are so many people I owe a thank-you for their help and encouragement with this project, and who have been supportive of my writing in general. I want to give a huge thanks to my family, my critique partners, my editors, and my wonderful publicity and marketing folks at Entangled Publishing. A big thanks to Katie Clapsadl, who is a special sort of publicity wizard and all around awesome person. And a big thank you to Barbara Rogan, who has not only helped me become a better writer, but has been amazingly supportive throughout my journey.

A special thank-you to Kerry Vail and Regan Summers for last-minute reads and fabulous advice. My mother for never faltering in her faith. My husband for supporting me in the scary decision to go for this writing dream. Erin Molta and KL Grady for their always fabulous editing. And Robin Haseltine for her wonderful editing as well. Thanks to all of my friends and fellow writers for their support and kindness.

Last, but certainly not least, a huge thank you goes out to all of my readers.

About the Author

CPA-turned-romance-author Tiffany Allee used to battle spreadsheets in Corporate America, and now concentrates on her characters' battles to find love. Raised in small-town Colorado, Tiffany currently lives in Phoenix, AZ, by way of Chicago and Denver. She is happily married to a secret romantic who tolerates her crazy mutterings.

She writes about ass-kicking heroines and the strong heroes who love them. Her work includes the suspense-driven *Otherworlder Enforcement Agency* series which revolves around a group of paranormal cops solving crimes and finding love, and *Don't Bite the Bridesmaid*, a lighthearted paranormal romance (Entangled Publishing).

Tiffany has an MBA in accounting and nearly a decade of experience in corporate finance. All super useful stuff for a writer who spends far too much time trying to figure out fun ways to keep her characters apart, and interesting ways to kill people (for her books—of course!). http://tiffanyallee.com